P9-CJT-203

DISNEY
THE
LITTLE
MERMAID

Against the Tide

Copyright © 2023 Disney Enterprises, Inc. All rights reserved.

Published by Disney Press, an imprint of Buena Vista Books, Inc.
No part of this book may be reproduced or transmitted in any form
or by any means, electronic or mechanical, including photocopying,
recording, or by any information storage and retrieval system,
without written permission from the publisher.

For information address Disney Press,
1200 Grand Central Avenue,
Glendale, California 91201.

Printed in the United States of America
First Hardcover Edition, April 2023
1 3 5 7 9 10 8 6 4 2
FAC-004510-23055
Library of Congress Control Number: 2022936731
ISBN 978-1-368-07722-4

Visit disneybooks.com

SUSTAINABLE FORESTRY INITIATIVE   Certified Sourcing
www.sfiprogram.org
SFI-01681

Logo Applies to Text Stock Only

Elle, J., author.
Against the tide

2023
33305257525950
ca   06/26/23

DISNEP

THE

LITTLE
MERMAID

Against
the Tide

By J. Elle

DISNEP PRESS
LOS ANGELES • NEW YORK

For Amelia,
who I carry with me every moment of every day

Chapter
1

Five Days Until the Coral Moon

Ariel rolled in her clamshell bed with buckling anticipation. She dug her nails into the seaweed covers pulled tight to her chin and looked for the glimpse of morning sunrays that would stream into her room in mere moments, officially marking the day she would get to leave home for the first time.

Click. The clock worm ticked his spindly body to the half shell, signaling the start of the day, and Ariel barreled out of bed as if there were springs under her tail. A hum spilled from her lips, and Ariel swayed along to the melody as she moved through her room. She paused for a glance at the polished glass above her dresser, straightening her back. She twisted her lips, perplexed. She wasn't sure what she expected to see, but something different, surely.

The next day, she, like each of her sisters before her, would be deemed Protector of her very own sea territory. And she was to be assigned the *best* territory of all, the one where she lived—Carinae! Their father's castle, where she had grown up, was in low-sun Carinae, but its boundaries stretched *far* across the ocean. The high-sun side of Carinae, where her headquarters as Protector would be, was altogether different, she had read. It was rumored to have true turquoise water and fish in every color of the rainbow.

Growing up, she had not been allowed to travel far beyond her father's castle. Oh, how she hoped being its Protector would mean she could explore its vastness. She closed her eyes, imagining endless undiscovered wonders and all manner of adventure she could unfurl. Ariel had hardly been able to sleep the past few weeks, her excitement growing as each new day brought her closer to her Protector Ceremony.

The ceremony happened the year a member of the royal family turned fifteen, and it was traditionally held four days before the annual Coral Moon Festival, when the moon turned a shade of pink so rare and so beautiful that it was said to bring *luck* to anyone who viewed it.

Ariel leaned on her desk. Its whalebone was soft to the

touch, and she couldn't help admiring the beautiful detail the royal carpenter had carved into its legs. The desk was a gift from her father: a stately piece of furniture for her to do all her Protector business, which would include creating new territory guidelines, meeting with important figures in the community, hosting events, and a whole slew of other responsibilities to those in Carinae.

She had studied as much as she could about what she would need to do as a Protector. Her father, King Triton, had said she'd learn much "on the job," and it must have been a *big* job, because her sisters were so busy with their duties in their respective territories that she hadn't seen them in . . . *years*. Mala had left over a decade ago, followed by Indira and Caspia. The others had trickled out over time until Ariel had found herself the only princess in the castle. Though her sisters were good at avoiding each other. So perhaps it wasn't busyness that kept them away.

Ariel dusted her desk and straightened the things on it: a cockle she'd found once that was just too interesting to leave behind; a jar of squid ink; a stack of sticky Pitonian seaweed perfect for writing notes, which her sister Perla had gifted her before she'd left for her own duties in the Piton Sea when Ariel was just a little fry. She stacked and restacked the scrolls on her desk, almost all of them about Carinae and all the areas she had yet to see. She'd churned her nervous energy these past few weeks between lessons on sea history and reading up on social etiquette, the proper way to host dignitaries, and what sorts of sanctions her sisters had put in place to better their territories for the seafolk there. She wanted to learn all she could, and she looked forward to exploring every nook and cranny of her territory with any free moment she had.

Just the thought sent a shiver of excitement up her arms as she moved back to her mirror. Her bonnet, woven together with silky strands of seaweed, was half off, as it always was each morning. She tossed it, letting her auburn locs, well oiled with sap from misaju-water coconuts, spill down her back. She posed again in the reflective glass, lengthening her torso, then grabbed the fine blue sea whip shawl she would don with her headpiece for the ceremony in a few days. She ran her fingers over its soft coral fibers. They'd been woven together strand by strand for weeks to make the ceremonial garment. Its little sleeves were adorned with pearl beadwork to match the ceremonial headpiece, also made just for her. Both were simply stunning.

"Nice to meet you. I'm . . ." She cleared her throat. *Too high.* She had to come across as serious. Her father always sounded so deliberate and authoritative when he spoke. She straightened herself, and the words came out stronger this time. "It's a pleasure to meet you. I'm Ariel, Protector of Carinae. How can I be of help?" She dangled her hand in the water, imagining someone taking it in greeting.

She carefully set aside her ceremony shawl and made her way down the halls. The castle came to life with the squeaking of shells being cleaned and windows being opened. Urchins dragged their bodies along the bone walls to polish them, while opah and tuna shuffled back and forth to heat the lower-level rooms.

Ariel frowned impatiently as she was caught in a corridor traffic jam caused by a school of tidying-up wrasse, ushered along by Julia, the head housekeeper.

"Good morning, Julia!" Ariel's frown turned into a smile as she spotted the matronly arthropod who diligently tidied her bed each morning. Ariel really could make her own bed. She just preferred to fill her tummy first. She'd tell Julia not to worry about it, that she would get to tidying her room later in the day, but she knew the dutiful housekeeper wouldn't hear of it.

The daughter of the king's room should be pristine, Julia would say.

Ariel kept moving. The idea of her entire sea present at her ceremony was beyond thrilling. They could make enough room for everyone, surely. She descended a tunnel to the lower floor of the castle, swishing faster down the corridor, eager to get her father on board with her idea during their morning meal.

Ariel found her father, King Triton, in the dining area, brooding over a kelp scroll with the morning reports from his Royal Guard.

"Morning, Father."

King Triton looked up from his reading and smiled.

"Is that my baby girl?" he asked. He put down his scroll and swam over from the table to spin her around.

"Dad, come on," Ariel said. "I'm fifteen, not five."

"You may as well still be five to me."

She indulged her father, convinced by the smile lines hugging his eyes. He was proud, and that tugged Ariel's lips into a grin. When he finally released her, she fell into one of the empty clamshell seats and filled her plate.

"Can you really eat all that?" Sebastian, one of her father's most trusted advisors, tapped his claws with narrowed eyes from where he sat on the table. "Wherever will you put it?"

"Good morning, Sebastian. And yes! Watch me." She shoved a full bite in her mouth, savoring the salted sea fennel.

"A healthy appetite is never a bad thing." Her father winked and pushed Ariel another plate of fennel.

"Yes, yes." Sebastian shrugged. "It is true. They grow like

seaweed, Sire. I remember when Mala was sitting there no taller than the fork of your trident. And now the last one will have her very own sea."

As Sebastian spoke, Ariel gathered her courage. "Actually, about that—I wanted to see if we could talk about the guest list for my ceremony."

Her father dabbed the corners of his mouth. "The guest list?" He slid another bite into his mouth. "What about the guest list, exactly?"

She cleared her throat, readying herself. "I'd like to send an open invitation to the entire territory."

Ariel wasn't sure who all had been invited to her ceremony besides the usual dignitaries, but she'd made up her mind late the night before: she would convince Father to open her ceremony for all Carinaeans, Sea Monsters and merfolk alike, to attend.

Long in the past, before Ariel or even her father had been alive, the Mer–Monster Treaty had been put in place in order to bring peace between merfolk and Sea Monsters, the creatures who lived in the deepest parts of the ocean. It was decided that Sea Monsters would be restricted from leaving their designated seas, of which there were seven in total, as a security measure. The Treaty also called for each sea to have a Protector, a merperson descended from the royal bloodline, to help oversee its affairs, and a Resident, a Sea Monster representative, to work with the Protector to mediate any disputes within territories and keep the peace.

Normally, Sea Monsters were excluded from the Protector Ceremonies, but Ariel wanted to be the type of leader who considered all the creatures in her territory, not just the ones that were like her.

"The *entire* territory?" Father's brows kissed in confusion.

"Yes," Ariel replied. She had spent most of the night reciting the things she planned to say to persuade her father to agree to her plans to open up the guest list. She had anticipated her father's pushback. He *would* push back. He could be notoriously rigid on the topic of Sea Monsters. He was even wary of the few Sea Monster Residents, despite having chosen them himself.

"You don't understand what you're asking," her father said.

"Is there not enough room?"

"We've a whole ocean. Room isn't the issue."

"Then what is?" Ariel asked

Father sat silent, a heaviness tugging at his shoulders and his thin lips.

Ariel could tell she would need backup to convince her father. She looked around for Usengu, the Sea Monster who acted as her father's right hand, Overseer of Residents. He was the only Sea Monster her father undoubtedly trusted, and he acted as Ariel's honorary uncle. But he was nowhere to be found. Ariel vaguely remembered Julia mentioning to her at some point that he had been planning to head to the Protector palace, on the other side of Carinae, early to help with the ceremony preparations. Sebastian was her next best bet. "Sebastian, you see what I'm saying, right?"

Sebastian's beady eyes darted between them. He knew something. He always knew something. She narrowed her eyes at him.

"There's no way inviting everyone is a good idea. I agree with your father," Sebastian said.

"Of course you do," she muttered.

"Ariel, it's not safe. Your territory won't have a Resident picked until after your ceremony. And we can't have just anyone showing up. Something like that is just reckless. This is why . . ." Her father rubbed his temples with a deep sigh. "Darling, you've only confirmed what I've been worried about."

"Worried?"

"This is a lot for you to take on by yourself."

Ariel felt her insides smush in panic. He was having doubts about her being Protector?

"Your sisters—" the king went on.

"My sisters did the same thing after they turned fifteen!" Ariel interrupted. "Why should I be any different?"

"I know making decisions like this can be hard, which is why I think now is a good time to tell you that you won't have to do it alone," King Triton said. "I have asked Sebastian to oversee you as Protector for the first year. Anything you need to decide you can defer to him, and he can run things by me as needed."

What!

"Father, that's not fair," Ariel said. "Did any of my sisters have to do that?"

"That isn't important."

She rammed an accusing finger toward Sebastian. "You went along with this? Tell him it's not fair!"

"Now, now." King Triton took her hand. "Don't beat up on Sebastian. This was my decision. He should probably get going anyhow. There's much work to do to prepare for the trip at dusk." He turned to Ariel. "And we won't soil such an exciting day with a disagreement. You'll still get to do plenty of exciting things." He lowered his eyes. "*Under* supervision."

"I—" Ariel opened her mouth to protest again.

"That's the end of it."

Whatever warmth Ariel had felt for her father that morning had dried up like a jellyfish in the sun. Her father's thin lips left room for no argument. She sank in her chair. It was supposed to have been an amazing day, but so far all she felt was disappointment.

"Yes, Father," Ariel said. She was gathering another bite of her food when a server slid a shiny dome toward her.

"A gift for you, Princess."

"Me?"

Ariel glanced at her father, and he shrugged, but something about the pinch of his lips made her narrow her eyes in suspicion.

"Father, what are you . . ." She lifted the dome to find a single kelp scroll addressed in swirly writing to her. Father's royal flock of loons took messages from various parts of the sea. Ariel could count on one hand how many times they'd brought her a message. She unfurled it.

Formal responses have been received from
Princesses Mala, Karina, Indira, Caspia, and Perla.
All have confirmed they will be in attendance
at Princess Ariel's Protector Ceremony.

Her sisters! They were coming for her ceremony!

Well, most of them. Tamika's name wasn't on there, but that was typical.

Ariel swam up from the table so hurriedly, her fins

knocked over her seat. "They're all going to be there!" The sinking feeling in the pit of her stomach over Sebastian's being her babysitter soothed some. "Thank you, Father. Thank you so much."

"They're excited to see you, darling. And with it being so close to . . ." His words trailed off. But Ariel didn't need him to finish. That time of the year was always hard for their family, but being deemed Protector was simply too special to miss. Ariel hugged the scroll tight to herself, relieved to know her sisters thought so, too.

The day wore on, and Ariel made preparations for the trip. She was still annoyed over Father ordering she be watched over by Sebastian like a child. Ariel plopped on her clamshell bed before convincing herself to get up and finish packing. Dusk would be upon them soon. Sebastian had already knocked multiple times to see that she wouldn't hold the royal caravan up. She would be ready on time. He was apparently taking his duties as her supervisor seriously.

The trip to the high-sun side of Carinae shouldn't take long, but she intended to stay there a while, so she needed to pack quite a few items. She'd be there at least a week for the ceremony and the Resident selection process, and then to get acquainted with the creatures unique to her territory.

Her father wouldn't let her invite everyone to her ceremony, but he couldn't stop her from getting to know the Carinaeans in her territory once she was actually their Protector. When she eventually returned home to the castle, she'd toggle back and forth between both places, she supposed. She couldn't imagine just being gone forever like her sisters. As mad as she was at her father and as excited as she was about exploring the rest of her territory, his castle was still her home.

A rap on her door startled her.

"I'm almost done, Sebastian, I swear," she called over her shoulder.

Her door creaked open and her father's face appeared. "Might I come in?"

His expression was apologetic, but the frustration from their earlier conversation tangled like a nest of seaweed in Ariel's chest. She gestured for him to enter but turned her attention back to her packing, not ready to face him. Why couldn't he see she was going to be really good at this? She could handle it. A heavy hand settled on her shoulder, but she shrugged it away.

"Listen," King Triton's voice boomed in that way it did, strong and gentle all the same. Her father was wise and careful with decisions. But he could be shortsighted and stubborn, too. If his mind was made up, it was as rigid as sunken steel. She huffed a breath before turning to face him.

"I just don't understand," she said. "Why won't you let me do this by myself?"

He sighed. "Ariel, that side of Carinae is largely unknown, and you don't have a Resident assigned yet. Sending you out there makes your ol' dad a bit nervous. Your sisters grew up . . . a bit faster, savvier, because—"

Ariel could see the memory of Mother hugged around his words, his tone, his posture, like a ghost.

He thinks I'm naive, Ariel thought. She could have shaken his shoulders if he hadn't been so tall. But instead, she pulled on his arm, and her father looped his through hers in that way he did, patting her hand dotingly.

"I'm a king, Ariel. I have to look at all the factors involved. Once you get *really* settled in your territory, I'll call Sebastian off. You have my word. You know . . ." He nudged her with his elbow. "I saved it special for you. I knew you'd love it."

He was right about that. The high-sun side of the Carinae Sea was wondrous, and so much of it was still undiscovered.

"I'm actually really looking forward to exploring it," she said, managing a smile.

Her father smiled back. "You sound like your mother."

Ariel wasn't sure what to say to that.

Her mother had died when Ariel had been very little, but she didn't know many details. All her father had told her was that she had gone out for a swim one day and was killed in an accident. The older Ariel got, the more questions she had. But each time she broached the subject, her father got uneasy, or her sister's mood would shift. Mother's death hovered over her family like a thunderous storm.

She could hardly remember her mother's face. But she could still recall the coconut scent of her hair, the way it shone auburn like hers. And her eyes, big, beautiful, and brown. Ariel stroked the purple pebble set in a woven bracelet on her wrist, its twine almost all worn. It had been a gift from her mother, and she never took it off. But though Ariel had these faint recollections of her mother, what she had actually been like was a mystery to Ariel—one she didn't spend much time on. She'd made up her mind long before to drop her queries and just be sunshine for the family. That was what they needed.

"Just don't go off exploring without permission, and make sure you never go alone." Triton rubbed his temples. "The bottom line is, I don't know that side of Carinae well enough to send my daughter there to do this job on her own. At first, at least. It's dangerous."

"If you don't know what's there, how do you know it's dangerous?" Ariel asked.

He sighed, exasperated. "It's unknown, Ariel. Listen to yourself. It's not like here. It's—"

"Different and wondrous and thrilling and—"

"You're *not* going alone!" His temper had flared, his voice firm. "I'm sorry to disappoint you, Ariel. We are going soon. Leave your bags in the corridor so Julia can get them."

Ariel nodded, chilly disappointment rolling off her in waves.

Her father headed toward the door before turning back. "Ariel, in time, when you're a bit older, you'll come to thank me. You'll see."

"Doubt it," Ariel muttered when her door clicked shut. She grabbed the note she'd gotten at their morning meal from her desk, soaking in its words again. She might be forced to be babysat for an *entire* year, but at least she still had one thing to look forward to at her ceremony.

Chapter 2

Five Days Until the Coral Moon

The foyer of the castle was filled with bristling revelry, and Ariel put on her best excited expression. Though, judging by Sebastian's double take at her when she joined the royal caravan, she must not have been terribly convincing.

"It is a sad day to see that bottom lip stuck out like that, Princess," the crab said. He was loyal to Father through and through, but Ariel knew he cared somewhere deep down. Sebastian nudged her with his claw, but the gesture didn't do a thing for her mood.

You'll see your sisters in a matter of hours, she thought to cheer herself. But Father's stern words fluttered through her mind like tumbling coral.

"If your father thinks I need to be helping, it's the right thing, child," Sebastian continued. "You'll see. The king knows best."

Ariel gave him a tight smile in response and swam past him to a cluster of translucent fins hung over branches like a strand of sea grapes. She grabbed the one with her name etched on one of the scales. They were shiny where the others were worn and discolored. She should be excited, getting to use her freshly fitted FastFins for the first time. She slipped the shimmery material, sized just for her, over her tail and watched it melt into her scales, giving them an iridescent sheen.

FastFins let them travel at ten times their normal speed. She could outswim the swiftest dolphin and cover more water than a whale in a fraction of the time. With as vast as their kingdom was, they had to have a way to get around quickly. Such a tool was a great responsibility. They even had their very own secured storage area in the royal armory, and it was a rule that they *must* be returned and cleaned each time they were used. As he had with everything else big and important, her father had made her wait until her ceremony trip to try hers out.

"You have everything you need?" her father chimed as he secured a final strap down on their things, which were packed into a collection of mollusk and oyster shells. Her father had someone to do that for him, she knew, but it was like him to want to handle things himself. Ariel didn't want to look at him, her face still stained with her disappointment. Instead, she nodded quickly and hoped that was enough.

Sebastian was corralling the royal entourage of clam carriages, each loaded down with storage shells from the kitchens, decorations from the royal designers, and a mountain of kelp-woven bags stuffed with their items, into an orderly procession. The Royal Nkatafish was on hand to certify things once the ceremony was over and make it official. All appeared to be in order.

"Get along now or we'll get a late start," said Julia as she swam over to Ariel. "But there is something I would like to give you first."

She held out a set of bound scrolls.

"What is—" But the letters on the first one answered her curiosity. On a turquoise expanse of wide ocean wreathed with colorful coral and speckled with sea creatures sparkled the title HIGH-SUN CARINAE.

"I found this in your mother's private library. I wasn't sure if you'd see it," Julia said. She dabbed at her eyes with her jackknife claws. "I'm so proud of you."

Ariel squeezed her maid's claw. She was so glad Julia would be there with her.

"Thank you so much, Julia. I'll read every word, I prom-ise," she said. She *was* excited about her territory. She would focus on that and her sisters, and give this arrangement her dad had worked out her best shot.

Ariel joined the front of the caravan with the others already strapped into their shimmery Fins. Sebastian didn't have FastFins, so he was tucked into Father's satchel with the other finless seafolk accompanying them on the journey. FastFins were tricky and took a long time to make; forged by the king's trident, they required a special material that could be found only at certain times of the year. So only a few mer-folk, like members of the royal family, received them. Ariel wiggled her tail to be sure that her FastFins were working, and her scales shone silver for a split second. But otherwise, her tail looked normal.

Around her, the preparations came to a close as the cara-van readied to be off. Ariel took a second to take in the scene.

"All this . . . for me."

It was a lot of work putting together the Protector Ceremony, Ariel realized. She felt a twinge of something twist in her insides. She didn't feel more mature; she cer-tainly didn't have more control over her life. But looking at the orchestra of preparations drumming around her, she couldn't deny one thing—being deemed Protector was a big deal.

The pressure of her new role hit her at full force. Would she do it well? She bit her lip. Would her father be proud? Who knew? He was so hard to please. Would her mother be proud? The thought made her feel . . . funny. Why had she thought of such a question? One she could never have an answer to.

Ariel slung her bag over her shoulder. Whatever the future held, her life as usual would never be the same. The knot in her stomach twisted again, this time in that way that made her lips tug in a smile.

"Are we ready?" her father called, joining her at the front of the procession.

Ariel pulled her hair back with a seagrass tie and rolled her shoulders. There was something electrifying about that. *Change.* It was not the unknown she hungered for, but something new was on the horizon. And that was exciting.

"I'm ready." She held the bound scrolls Julia had given her tighter to herself as the caravan jutted into motion, ready to make the most of whatever lay ahead.

The high-sun side of Carinae didn't look like anything she'd seen on her scrolls. It was magnificently more stunning. No re-creation could ever do it justice. The water gleamed a deep bluish green, the ocean floor vibrant with colorful algae. They passed coral reefs more radiant than she'd ever seen and water so clear she had to blink to be sure it was real. A duo of trumpet fish had arranged themselves not far from what would be her Protector palace, a petite, fancy building surrounded by a tall stone wall, to announce her arrival with cheer.

A chorus of butterfly fish sang along as Ariel waved to them all. She'd met many different seafolk at her father's castle, but everyone here seemed so exuberant and thrilled to see the royal family making a home in *their* part of the ocean. Fish, merfolk, and creatures lurking in shadows flanked the pathway to the palace, forming a long aisle.

"Welcome to High Sun, Princess!"

The shouts from the crowd warmed Ariel's cheeks. Colorful tunicates bunched in bouquets lay atop the gate, and bits of seaflora flew at them like confetti as they swam through. The gate locked behind them, and Ariel froze stiff at the opulent walls around her. The palace was nestled in a stunning cluster of coral with deep reds and soft peaches. Its towering walls were smooth like bone. Leaves in all shapes and sizes wreathed a glass dome above them all. Shards of shiny glass were woven into nets slung overhead, which scattered the sunlight like a night sky in the daytime.

Ariel gasped. She was taking it all in when she bumped into a firm something.

"So what do you think? Beautiful, right?" Her father rubbed her shoulders.

"I . . . I've never seen anything like it," Ariel managed, still in awe.

"And I take it that's a good thing?" the king asked.

Ariel faced him, warmth swirling through her like a cyclone. "Father, it's the *best* thing!"

After the caravan came to a halt in front of the palace and her father gave her the okay to look around, Ariel swam down the narrow corridors to locate her room. She found it easily enough. It was spacious with plentiful shelves and lots of room to ready and style herself. It had a great big window facing west, through which shone the orange-pink hue from the sky far above their world.

Servants brought in her things behind her. She itched to help them, but she couldn't tear her eyes away from her new second home. The walls were smooth bone, like the foyer, but dotted with holes and illuminated with the glow of jellyfish. Twisted florals and beautiful shells in all sizes and shapes adorned the walls. It wasn't grand or fancy, but it had character. A story in every nook and cranny.

On a small desk, Ariel found a bouquet of bright neon sea lilies next to a tear of seaweed scribbled on in shimmery squid ink. *Proud of you,* it said. She turned it over and found Usengu's name.

"Who's all here?" someone said from the hall.

Ariel's brows pinched at the familiar voice. Perla! Her sisters had started to arrive!

She barreled out of her room and straight into her sister, smothering her in a hug. Perla's blue hair was pulled back in a long braid.

"Ari!" she exclaimed, her red tail swishing.

Ariel hated that nickname, but bit her tongue. She wouldn't let the first thing out of her mouth after seeing her sister in so long be negative. After all, her sisters were at each other's throats enough. Growing up in a castle with six other girls had been no joke.

"How have you been? You're the real deal now!" Perla had always been Ariel's closest sister. She was the last to leave the castle, and she visited the most often. But even before she had been Protector, they had talked the most, had the most in common, and for whatever reason, usually got in the most trouble together. Which was its own sort of bonding experience.

"You have to tell me everything I missed." Perla hugged Ariel again, twirling them in a circle and drumming up a cloud of bubbles around them. "How has prep been going? What was it like using your FastFins for the first time? What mermen do you have your eye on?" Perla added a sly smile to that last part, and Ariel felt her cheeks flush.

"Okay, okay." Ariel glanced over her shoulder at the corridor growing smaller, now jam-packed with servants unloading their belongings. "Let's go to my room!"

Perla always had been able to make her smile. Ariel missed all her sisters, but if she was honest, she missed Perla most. The last time she'd spent an abundance of time with her sister was right before Perla donned her FastFins for her own ocean assignment, which had happened right before their mother had passed. Perla was back and forth from her sea to their father's castle every several moons over the first few years, but eventually her visits tapered off. All of Ariel's sisters had come back to the castle a few times after their mother's death . . . at first.

Except for Tamika.

Ariel hadn't seen Tamika since the day their mother had passed. There were all sorts of whispers in the kingdom about her sister, but Ariel refused to believe any of them. She did wonder what kept her sister *so* busy she could never visit. But time had swept away and drowned the memories of Tamika in the castle like a riptide. No one even mentioned her anymore.

Inside her room, Ariel spilled to Perla about Sebastian's being her babysitter and her disappointment, but being pleasantly surprised with how nice things were on this side of Carinae.

"Oh, come on, this is Father we are talking about. Mister Controlling. And this far from his castle, his youngest fry . . . I'm not surprised he's assigned his second set of eyes. You better be careful or he'll have Usengu watching over you, too."

"That might not be so bad," Ariel said. *Usengu is so much more fun than Mister Crabby.* "I just wanted him to believe I could do this."

"It's not you. It's the Sea Monsters here he's probably worried about." Perla shuddered, her expression darkening for a moment before her bright smile returned.

"I guess," said Ariel. "But there are Sea Monsters in every territory."

"Yeah, but you don't have a Resident yet. It takes time to find the right Sea Monster for the job, and that buffer really helps keep us separate from them. Safe from them."

"It seems a bit overkill to me."

"You're in for a big job, Ari. You might feel different once you've started," Perla said. "There are so many different seafolk, and everyone can have different ideas about how things should be done. I know I didn't feel fully prepared to manage everything when I started, is all I mean. Thank goodness for Usengu." Perla smiled, removing a curl from Ariel's face. "Just . . . focus on getting through the ceremony tomorrow for now."

Ariel couldn't remember the last time she'd felt so excited.

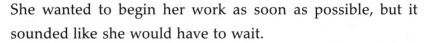

She wanted to begin her work as soon as possible, but it sounded like she would have to wait.

"Have you talked to Mala or any of the others?" Ariel asked, changing topics. Perla's smile turned into a frown.

"You know we don't really talk."

"I mean, I know. But have you tried reaching out?"

Perla sighed, fussing with her hair in the glass next to Ariel's wardrobe. "Okay, little miss peacemaker. No, I haven't. Don't judge me. I just don't have—"

"Time, I know." Ariel didn't buy it. But she didn't press. She would let nothing ruin this moment. "I—"

Bang.

Ariel's and Perla's eyes met, narrowed with concern. "What was—"

Bang.

Another, louder this time.

"That sounds like—" Ariel started.

"Doors slamming," Perla finished.

Tousled voices shouting one over the other grew louder, punctured by a few more bangs, and Ariel's buoyed excitement sank like an anchor.

The rest of her sisters had arrived.

And they were fighting. As usual.

Ariel had known this trip would be a challenge, but she hadn't expected bickering from the outset.

"Well," Ariel said, "we should go out there and see what's going on."

"Speak for yourself," said Perla. "I'm going to find my room and unpack."

"Come on . . ."

"Nope. I'll follow you to the ends of the sea, sister. But not into a den of our sparring sisters. Even I have my limits." Perla laughed, shoving Ariel playfully, who chuckled. But it was more disappointing than anything else. Ariel had to think of something. Something to start them off on the right fin. Something so exciting and meaningful they couldn't help having a good time.

Perla left for her room, and Ariel twisted her hair around her finger as she swam down the hall. A passing servant informed her that Indira and Caspia had arrived and would be staying in the same quarters. Connected at the hip, those two. They usually finished each other's sentences.

Before Ariel could duck in and say hello to them, she spotted Mala, her long dark hair swaying at her waist, as beautiful as ever. Suddenly Ariel knew whose shell door had clattered so loudly against the bone walls. Indira and Caspia were always at odds with Mala. Ariel swam toward her sister, who was lugging a too-heavy seagrass-woven bag into her room, and she couldn't help a grin.

Mala was always the one they could look up to for an

example of how things should be done. She was good at *everything* without even trying. It was easy to be envious of someone like that, which Ariel guessed was her other sisters' problem. But Ariel missed Mala too much to be jealous. If anything, she wanted to learn all she could from her. It was Mala who had come back to the castle for a short trip once when Ariel was a small fry and taught her how to write her letters on kelp. When Ariel had managed to complete her first scroll, Mala was so proud she'd swum her down to the kitchens right then and had the royal chef make her favorite seatreat to celebrate.

"Mala!" Ariel called.

"Relle!" Mala grinned, and deep dimples dug into her cheeks.

Each of her sisters had a name for her. She really just preferred Ariel. But that was the least of her worries at the moment.

"Let me help," Ariel said, lifting the bag with a grunt. What had Mala packed in this thing?

"Thanks." Her sister's brown eyes settled on her, and they oozed with glee. There was a warmth to her, a glow, and though Ariel hadn't seen her in a long while, it was distinct.

"What's up with you?" she asked.

Mala flushed. "What do you mean?"

"You just look so . . . happy."

"I'm just excited to see you!" Mala's dimples deepened. She gazed around. "Is Karina here? I want to ask if she'll braid my hair for your ceremony tomorrow." She squeezed Ariel's arm, and Ariel's lips split in a huge smile. *This is really happening.*

"I don't think she's arrived yet."

"Soon, I bet," Mala said. She cupped Ariel's cheek. "Gosh, you've gotten so old. I wish Mother were here to see this."

Ariel squeezed her hand. Mala was the first to become a Protector and had been the closest to their mother. When she left for her sea, she'd packed up three entire bags of keepsakes from things she and Mother had done together. She refused to leave a single memory behind. And to think that when Mala had finally come to visit, she found bickering.

The fighting among her sisters had started after Mother died. Ariel's father had told her that where the halls had once been filled with laughter and their morning forays into the gardens, their mother's passing had filled the corridors with contention and heavy silence. The topic of Mother's death always made Ariel's insides feel weird, but other than that, she was fine. After all, she had been so young when her mother had passed, it made sense that her death hadn't really affected her. Her sisters were a different story.

Ariel set her jaw. She wouldn't let her sisters spend the entire week at each other's throats. No, that wasn't going to be how they started this visit. Ariel would make sure they had a great trip. But how?

With Mala's words about her mother on her mind, an idea hit Ariel, and she fixed her posture with determination as she helped her sister unpack her things. The rest of her siblings would arrive soon, and before any more doors slammed, Ariel knew just the thing they could do together to put them all on the same team.

Chapter 3

Five Days Until the Coral Moon

Each sea had erected a memorial to the queen shortly after her untimely death. It was nice to know so many wanted to remember her. And Ariel couldn't think of a better place to remind her sisters that they were a family.

It took a full turn of the shell before the rest of her sisters arrived. Once they did, Ariel visited each of their rooms. The evening was half over by the time she was able to convince each of them to join her for a trip to the Carinaean memorial a few whalebones away from the palace. She suspected the only reason any of them were on board was because she'd said it was the one thing she wanted as a gift for her Protector Ceremony. When she put it that way, the protests quieted, and eventually, they came around.

Ariel hung in the foyer as her sisters gathered, while Father pulled at his beard, watching from the landing of the upper floor. She could tell he was reconsidering letting them go out, but he'd gone over the directions to the memorial hundreds of times, and it wasn't very far. Plus they'd all be together.

"Get going so you're back before it's too late," the king said.

"We'll be fine, Father." Ariel rolled her eyes. She was only a day from being deemed Protector of her very own sea. She should be allowed to travel out late at night.

King Triton made a face but didn't press and left them to it.

"Are we leaving yet? This is taking forever." Caspia picked at her nails, her light pink hair floating, and Indira nodded in agreement. Everyone's eyes moved to Ariel, awaiting instructions.

"Are we sure Tamika isn't coming?" she asked. She knew her name had not been on the scroll her father had given her, but she was hoping she still might come.

"Who?" Indira said.

Caspia snorted. "I heard she doesn't even live in Fracus

anymore. That she was trying to find a way to trade her tail for wings."

"Okay, that's not true and you know it," Mala said, shoving past them both. Perla rolled her eyes and folded her arms, and Ariel wished she hadn't said anything out loud. Just because Tamika had forgotten them didn't mean they had to forget her. But brooding over it with them wasn't going to bring about anything but more complaining.

"Ugh, I have a headache. Do we really have to do this, like, right now?" Karina asked, rubbing her arms to warm herself as the chill from her trip wore off. She'd only just arrived. Her sea was the farthest, far up north, and was notoriously cold. "Can't we go to the memorial in the morning? I'm beat."

Indira rolled her eyes. "Of course, Karina's had it the hardest, you know. All the way up there in that northern sea with its icicles and snow flurries. Such a miserable existence." She laid the back of her hand on her forehead in teasing, and Caspia cackled, punctuated with snorts. Perla chuckled, too.

"You try swimming through glacial temperatures!" Karina shoved Indira. "See how you like it."

"Oh, gosh, the dramatics, Karina, seriously," Perla sneered.

Perla and Karina bickered until their arguing was a loud clang in Ariel's ears. Those two could go on for days. Indira and Caspia egged it on, but they didn't get along with anyone.

"Seriously, guys? Come on!" But Ariel wasn't heard as their back-and-forth morphed into a full-on screaming match. She rubbed her temples and considered just going to her room—forgetting about the entire thing. She turned the purple pebble bracelet on her arm. No, she wouldn't give up that easily.

"Would you all just please stop!" Her shout ricocheted off the bone walls. Everyone's lips snapped shut, and she had their attention. Ariel turned to Karina, whose long lilac hair had fallen out of its ribbon during the argument. "I'm sorry the trip wasn't kind, but our schedule is full tomorrow. Can you please come? We're all back together for the first time in forever. The anniversary of . . . you know. It's in a few days. We should do this."

"She's right." Perla shouldered her bag, and Ariel squeezed her hand in thanks.

"Well, let's get on with it," Mala chimed in, always the sport. Indira, Caspia, and Karina nodded in agreement, still glaring at each other, and Ariel was thankful for the momentary truce. She gestured for them to follow and led the way out through the gates.

Most of the crowd of Carinaeans who had been clustered at the gates when they'd arrived had gone. However, they'd left mountains of colorful shells, bunches of seaflora tied with grass, and notes staked in the ground with sweet messages on them to welcome Ariel. A warmth tugged at her as she spotted a few stragglers affixing an armful of gifts to the rails of the gate.

"Thank you so much!" She waved, and Indira snatched her arm down.

"You don't even know them."

"They're friendly."

"You assume!" Indira said.

Goodness, Father has made them all so untrusting.

"Let's just go," Ariel replied.

The trip to the memorial was faster than Ariel had expected, but she tarried as long as she could, taking the sea in. She rarely left her father's castle for outings. Her usual day consisted of voice lessons, court etiquette practice, lunch in the reef garden, and more voice lessons, and when she could, she'd steal away to the royal library and drown herself in scrolls. King Triton was stingy with her time outside of the castle, so she lived vicariously through stories about what the sea was like outside of their palace walls.

Any time Ariel did manage to get away, she made sure to bring a keepsake back home with her. But nothing she'd seen by her father's palace could compare in wonder to her soon-to-be territory, whose beauty wasn't bound behind the gates of the palace. The journey to the memorial was a maze of low-lying reefs and tunnels, an adventurer's dream. The turquoise water and rainbow-colored flora made her eyes pop with delight. Schools of fish and towers of billowing seaweed in grainy textures made the short trip one of masterful discovery.

They'd come across so many seafolk she'd lost count. All manner of crustaceans, a few merfolk, a pink octopus, and so many fish in every color of the rainbow. Each fish she saw brandished their brightly colored tail at her as they passed, and it took a few doing that before she realized that was their way of waving. She swished her tail at the next few they met, and that got her toothy smiles. She nudged Perla to do the same, but her sister wasn't nearly as enthusiastic. At one point Ariel found herself peering so hard at a stunning orange-and-pink shell on a sea turtle that she almost swam right into a statue.

"You know," Karina said as they skirted a pile of debris, "as Protector you'll want to make sure you get rid of those. Dispose of them somewhere. That stuff from the surface is full of toxins."

Ariel gazed up at Karina's words, and the golden sun glittered in a ripple. She had always wondered what it was like up there out of the water. It was like a whole other ocean to be discovered. Could it really all be poison? Karina had a flair for the dramatic.

"I assigned the Sea Monsters in Saithe to collection duty,"

Karina continued. "They should be thankful for the work. Most wouldn't even deal with them."

If Sea Monsters needed something, it was their Resident's responsibility to appeal to Usengu, who would talk to the King. Or the Protector could step in.

Ariel had never understood the big deal over the Sea Monsters, but she also hadn't been born when the Treaty between Sea Monsters and merfolk was formed. *How does it go? "A monster and a mermaid ruled each of the seven seas . . . forbidden . . ." No, that isn't it.* The precise language escaped her; she hadn't studied it in sea history for ages. But the meaning was *known*. In addition to restricting Sea Monsters to their territories, it made it a crime for mermaids and monsters to ever commingle or abdicate their Protector or Resident roles for love or any other reason. It didn't sit right with her. She couldn't put her finger on exactly why, though, especially when that was the way it had always been.

Ariel and her sisters slowed as they stumbled upon a plaque affixed to a gate shrouded in kelp.

"I think this is the memorial," Ariel said.

Her sisters quieted, peering through the grates at the reality of what they were about to face. Ariel pushed the squeaky gate but hesitated, her insides in a knot. She'd visited a memorial just once; she and her father had gone to the one closest to his castle right after her mother had died. She had been too small to remember much from the trip. After that, each year Ariel had asked to go again, but her father always had a reason he didn't want to leave the castle.

"Well." Ariel took a deep breath. "Who is going to go in first?"

"This was your idea," Caspia snapped.

Ariel sighed. To her relief, Perla swam inside with the rest on her tail. A mermaid statue sat in the center of a reef with tiny fish poking in and around it. Flowy coiled hair shrouded the statue's face. Its arms were clasped, and carved stone made up a broad tail.

The memorial grounds were completely empty but for Ariel and her sisters. The ocean was never entirely quiet, but at that moment, all she could hear was her heart thumping.

"It looks so much like her." Mala swam closer to the statue, touching its features as if it were Mother. Indira and Caspia stuck to each other's side, but their usual pinched expressions were tempered.

"I remember Mother took me sun-watching once, and we were gone so long Father sent out a search party," Mala continued with a laugh, rubbing the inside of her wrists together, something mermaids only did when they felt a deep ache of sadness. Ariel wanted to go to her, comfort her, but she still couldn't move, and she wasn't sure why.

Something she couldn't find words for pinned her in place, and she hung back, loitering on the memorial perimeter.

"The night before my Protector Ceremony," Mala went on, "she told me to be like the sun. A light for all in my territory to see, illuminating the darkest places. At the time I didn't quite know what a Protector did. Father made it sound like an honorary title. But years later, of course, after Mother died, everything grew tenser. The beautiful part in all that is as I spent more time in Chaine, I began to see just how much actual good I could do. Mother's words only made more sense the more time went on."

A blossom of warmth rippled through Ariel at the thought of Mother's being there for their ceremonies. That sounded . . . nice. A knot stuck in her throat.

"It was so different before, wasn't it?" Karina asked, swimming to Mala's side. "Before . . . Father got so worried about everything."

"Yeah, after my ceremony, I used to visit you and father all the time, but then—" Perla chimed in but cut herself off, her voice cracking in a way it hadn't been earlier. "Well, it's been a while."

Karina looped her arm through Perla's, and Mala did the same. The three of them fawned over the statue's features, sticking closely together as if their very proximity could give each other strength. This was hard for them. Ariel's lips parted, but she wasn't sure what to say, so she closed them.

Karina's gaze was far off, remembering. "We'd go to this steep drop-off point near . . ."

"Glowrise Shore, right?" Mala said.

"Yeah!" Perla and Karina said at the same time.

"That's the spot," Mala said. "I remember. Jagged rocks with that smooth shaded area hugged in coral. We'd sit there and watch the sun rise or set, depending. Mother loved it."

Ariel tried to picture the place or recall if she'd ever been there. She tugged at her bracelet.

"Did she ever take me?" Ariel asked.

"Oh, yes, all the time," Mala said, gesturing for Ariel to join them. But Ariel held on to the gate.

"She'd strap you to her back and go," Indira said.

"You were a notorious escape artist, Fry," Caspia said with a snort.

"Did you all ever gather those bulbs from the kelp and—" Mala began.

"Turn them into a necklace!" Karina cut in.

"Oh my goodness, yes. I'd squish them to make the gooey insides come out," Perla said, and they all burst into laughter.

Ariel's gaze hit the ground. Her grip tightened on the gate. She had no idea what they were talking about.

"Mother used to hate that." Indira barreled over in laughter before joining the others around the statue.

"Speaking of those necklaces, I still have one somewhere," Mala said.

"No way!" Caspia said.

"Yep. I kept them." Mala smiled fondly. "Mother taught me my MerSong while we were weaving them."

MerSongs were something all of them had because of Mother's Gift of Voice. The Gift had been a wedding present for Mother from Triton. Their mother's voice had been said to hold a power over others, and she could mold that ability into different forms through song. As she taught the Song to others, it would confer the Gift. So the queen had composed unique melodies for each of her daughters, to give them a special ability to aid them in their time of need, gird them for their service in their territories, and remind them just how special each of them was in her very own way.

Perla's could paralyze everything in a half-whalebone radius, and Indira could heat the temperatures around her to a boil. Caspia could temporarily shrink anything or anyone with just a tune, while Mala could lull the most restless sea creature to sleep with a single note. Ariel couldn't remember what Tamika's song did, as she'd never had a chance to see her use it before she disappeared. Each of her sisters had a MerSong unique to her. Except Ariel. Mother had died before she could confer the Gift to Ariel.

"Come on over here. You all right?" Mala gestured for Ariel once again, and Perla reached for her, too. But Ariel's tail felt like it weighed a ton. She studied the statue's face, trying to picture her mother's actual features, but it conjured no memories, just wisps, as usual. Unlike her sisters, she couldn't latch on to anything that made her want to rub her wrists together, laugh, or even smile. All she felt was more questions swirling in her head.

"Yeah, I'm okay." *I think.*

"Oh, come on." Perla pulled Ariel toward them. "What would Father say if he could see us now?"

Ariel shifted uncomfortably. She'd hoped their grief would be what brought them together. But it was their memories with Mother. Their experiences. That was *their* bond, not hers. She hadn't known her mother the same way. And never would. The truth sank Ariel's heart like an anchor, a sensation she'd never felt before.

Her sisters spent the rest of the time at the memorial remembering Mother's quirks and reliving ridiculous blunders from when they were smaller, but Ariel couldn't muster the desire to join in.

She would never know who their mother had been, just

as she would never have a MerSong of her own. Ariel sagged against the gate, letting it hold her up. She spent the rest of her time at the memorial in silence, trying to shake off the odd feelings she was having and instead set her thoughts on her new territory and all that was to come.

Chapter
4

Four Days Until the Coral Moon

The rest of the evening was full of ceremony preparations, but to Ariel's relief, the tensions between
her sisters had eased. Once they got back from the
memorial, they'd all had their hair stripped, a process that
infused the hair with a stickiness that made it easier to hold
the headpiece each would wear in place. Ariel had been
soaked in floral-infused waters until her skin was softer than
a sea sponge. She and her sisters had even spent the night
in Ariel's room. They were up late telling stories about their
own Protector Ceremonies. Ariel had been surprised to hear

that their mother had escorted all of them down the aisle during their ceremonies.

Even after their conversations were over and her sisters' snores surrounded her, Ariel hardly slept a wink. The more she thought about the ceremony, the more nervous she felt. Going through the long processional aisle of dignitaries to make her way to the ceremony stage all by herself made her feel sick. Her father had to wait for her at the end of the aisle, as was tradition, so she'd be on her own.

But at least some traditions had been tweaked over the years. Apparently, when Mala had had her ceremony, the tradition had been to put a fish in your shawl pocket for luck. But the fish she was paired with got sick the day of the ceremony. So her housekeeper convinced a random fish from Mala's sea to fill in. It turned out Mala was allergic to its scales, and she spent the entire ceremony wiggling and itching. Ariel was grateful that custom was over.

From what she gleaned from Perla, the worst she would have to endure was her hair being done. Apparently, the hairdresser was heavy-handed, and Ariel was tender-headed. She winced in anticipation.

"It's your day!" Mala squealed once morning came, rubbing the crust from her eyes. "How do you feel?"

"I don't know. The same." Ariel glanced at her headpiece,

which had been hung just so to prevent its shell and pearl beading's being crushed. "I'm excited to get all done up."

"I'm proud of you, Relle. Ignore those worms in your tummy. You're going to be magnificent."

Am I that transparent?

As if reading her thoughts, Mala winked. "All right, I'm off to breakfast and some other things." She smiled slyly and swam up with a bounce in her gait. She was absolutely giddy. Ariel would try to channel some of that excitement to squash her nerves.

"Oh my gosh, your elbow." Indira dislodged Caspia's elbow from her side and shook her sister awake. "Geez, you sleep terribly."

"It's true, Caspia. You fell asleep on the chair and woke up on the floor." Ariel laughed. "You snore, too."

"I do not," Caspia said with a yawn as she sat up.

Indira made an awkward face, nodding. "You do, sis."

"Do not!"

"Hey, there are worse offenses," Perla said, laughing.

"I mean, hardly," Ariel said, poking fun at the sister who prided herself on never doing anything improper. It was too irresistible not to.

Caspia's jaw dropped. "This is an attack."

"At your denial, yes." Indira's retort sent everyone barreling over in laughter. Even Caspia's composure fractured, and she burst out snorting.

"Well, at least I don't drool in my sleep," she sassed back, undoing and redoing her hair.

"All right, all right. Fair." Indira wiped the corners of her mouth, still snickering.

Karina's eyes popped open when the noise woke her.

"Good morning. What time is it?" She stretched before untangling herself from her leafy covers, which had some-how wrapped themselves all the way around her tail.

"Thanks for staying the night." Ariel's skin tingled at the sight of her sisters all around her. She pinched herself, con-vinced she might actually be dreaming.

"Of course," Karina said, sitting up fully. "We were all ner-vous before our Protector Ceremonies. It's a big deal."

"I swear, every time I think about my ceremony I feel like I am going to be sick," Ariel said, letting her deepest wor-ries out unencumbered as soon as she knew her sisters were there for it. "What if I do something out of turn or make a fool of myself? What if my hair looks stupid?"

Perla touched her arm. Karina hugged her.

"We're here," Indira said, and Ariel warmed all over.

"You're going to be brilliant," Caspia added.

Ariel tried to exhale, but the breath caught tight in her chest. She so wanted to believe them. "Things have been so nice since visiting Mother's memorial, and I just . . ." Ariel wasn't sure what exactly she was trying to say, only that this togetherness soothed something in her that had been long buried. "I hope we can keep things like this. Not just today, but, like . . . always? Maybe we could make a Promise Pact?"

Promise Pacts were oaths sworn by the magic in Father's trident. The terms of the promise were stated in the presence of the trident holder, Father, and the trident's magic sealed it, making the Pact participants unable to break their word without deadly consequences.

"Uhhh, *always* is a long time." Perla pursed her lips. "I'm kidding!"

They all laughed.

"But that is a bit drastic," Indira said. "The weight of a Promise Pact isn't to be taken lightly. Our word will just have to be good enough."

She's right. Ariel sighed. She just wanted to do something to make it *officially* official—that they would agree to not fight anymore. She'd just have to trust they would follow through. That this time together meant as much to them as it did to her.

Ariel exhaled. She and her sisters dawdled a bit longer before Indira and Caspia insisted they all get up and get moving for the day. It would be a busy one. The ceremony traditionally began right after high sun, and they all had much preparing to do. Hair and nails and polishing their scales. Their headpieces had to be attached, which was an entire art that took at least two sets of fins. And everyone had to be fitted into their shawls and get themselves in place. As her sisters dispersed, Ariel's stomach rumbled. Mala had the right idea, she decided, and hurried down to the dining chamber.

The dining room was full of kelp delicacies, the chef's famous algaecakes, and all sorts of delicious treats. A line of servants filling their plates roped either side of the table. Ariel looked for Mala but didn't see her. Ariel had to have just missed her. She grabbed a few cakes and a bowl of seaweed before quickly finding a spot to fill her tummy while others passed by with doting smiles and notes of congratulation. So many sea creatures stopped by that she ended up saying "thank you" every other bite.

"Excited for today?" someone said from behind her.

The voice was warm; she knew it immediately. She turned in her seat. "Usengu!"

His thick dark tail curled in the water, as it did when he was excited. For a sea serpent, he was large, almost as big as she was. Usengu had been in the castle for as long as Ariel could remember. He was the closest sea creature to Father outside of the family, other than Sebastian. He was also the only Sea Monster Father seemed to trust.

Usengu used to work in the royal library, but after Mother

died, Father had folded in on himself; Usengu had taken on more and more responsibility to help, especially with the Residents, whom Father couldn't bring himself to deal with anymore. Usengu had worked hard to ensure Father had time to grieve. That was when they had grown really close. He'd brief Ariel on each day's schedule when Father was too heavy with sadness to pull himself out of bed. He'd make sure she was tucked in at night in those really dark days after Mother died. Usengu was as good as family.

Once he'd earned Father's trust by sharing tons of ideas about how to help keep the palace safe and tighten restrictions in the territories while maintaining good relationships with the seafolk there, Father had named him Overseer of Residents and the king's right hand. It had brought him relief to know at least that part of running his kingdom would chug along smoothly, thanks to Usengu's competence. He'd been a lifeline Father relied on since then.

"How are you, Princess?" Usengu asked. "Are you ready for today?"

"As ready as I'll ever be." She smiled, but her voice cracked on delivery.

"Don't be nervous. You will be radiant! This ceremony will be one no one forgets."

Usengu was like an uncle to her! And not nearly as on her case all the time as Sebastian. Ariel wondered . . .

"Usengu, is there any chance you could escort me through the procession during my ceremony?" she asked, biting her lip.

The Sea Monster's eyes widened. "Oh, that is so sweet, dear Ariel. I'm honored you'd think of me. How I wish I could." He patted her arm. "But I'll be behind the scenes making sure things go just right. Your father's all wound up today."

Her shoulders sank.

"There, there." He hugged around her with his fin, and she braced for the chill. As sweet as Usengu was, his fins were cold and slimy.

"We also wouldn't want to upset the merfolk," Usengu continued. "You know, with me being a Sea Monster and all."

Ariel wrinkled her nose. "That's nonsense!"

"At any rate, I don't think I can, my dear."

She sighed. It was worth a shot. Her earlier anxiety over swimming down the aisle by herself coursed through her.

"Deep breaths, Princess," Usengu said. "She would be so proud of you."

She. My mother. Any time something bugged her, everyone always assumed it pointed back to Mother. In fact, she was just really nervous about being up there—all those eyes on her and only her—alone. Ariel nodded at Usengu before Father entered in a bluster.

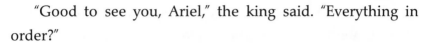

"Good to see you, Ariel," the king said. "Everything in order?"

She smiled. *Sunshine.* She didn't want to add on to his stress. "Yes, Father."

"Very good. If I might steal this one here." Her father thumb-pointed at Usengu. "Just the serpent I was looking for."

"Of course."

Father turned to Usengu, and Ariel returned her attention back to her half meal.

"I heard about renewed tension between merfolk and Sea Monsters back at the castle." Her father's voice dropped to a whisper, but Ariel's ears perked up. "Has any of that reached the high-sun side of Carinae?" Hard lines dug between Father's brow.

Tension? Here? Ariel thought with a frown. Everyone she'd seen was so happy. Their joy at her arrival shrouded the gate outside in colorful blooms.

"No, Sire, all is in order," Usengu said. "I've made sure. I met with the Residents from the other territories yesterday. They won't be attending the ceremony to keep a close eye on Sea Monsters in their seas. I've put the pressure on them to keep a firm fin on things." Usengu's expression deadened, and Ariel's heart leapt in her chest. This was serious.

"Very good." Her father's shoulders visibly sank. "Let's

hurry and get prospects for Residents in Carinae lined up. I want someone I trust in place before I return home."

Usengu and her father swam away, putting an end to her eavesdropping. Ariel tried her best to shove off Father's kingdom concerns and focus on her own. She wouldn't have an escort, it looked like. She'd just have to swim the procession aisle without one.

Mala had made it sound like the procession wasn't a big deal, and Mala was pretty much right all the time. Ariel huffed out a breath, tightening her fist as if her bare hand could hold on to the joy of the night before with her sisters. Everything would work itself out, and she'd be fine.

Ariel finished her meal and hurried upstairs to her room, where the hairdresser was waiting with Julia. Her housekeeper tickled her elbow and winked. Ariel couldn't help grinning from ear to ear. Julia smiled back, tiredness shading her expression. She looked stressed . . . more than usual, it appeared. Likely due to all the preparations. Ariel bit her lip. She must remember to make sure Julia took a nice long break once the Ceremony was over.

Her ceremonial shawl seemed to shine a richer, deeper blue than it had before, or perhaps Ariel was just more excited.

"Can I do the honor of draping it on you?" Perla was at the door.

"Please!"

Her sister helped her slip into the soft garment, which had arm cutouts. The hairdresser set out a brush and ornaments for her hair, and Julia helped apply some pink pigments to her lips and cheeks. Ariel twirled in the shawl once it was properly placed over her shoulders and took in her full appearance in the mirror.

"If Mother could see this . . ." Perla ran her fingers over the shawl's handwoven threads. "Her littlest Ariel with her very own ocean."

"She would be proud, right?" Ariel asked.

Perla spun Ariel in her grasp, her brows raised in disbelief. Ariel met her sister's eyes, fighting the urge to stare at her fins.

Where did that question come from? she wondered. Usengu's earlier comment must have gotten her thinking about it.

"What? Are you kidding me? She would be *so* proud!" Perla squeezed her hand and hugged her tight.

"Thanks for being here," Ariel said.

"Not just me, all of us. We knew we needed to be here for you in this way. Mala and Father coordinated the whole thing."

"I must thank her. I haven't seen her since this morning,

actually." The others she'd passed in the halls on the way to her room, or she'd overheard ruckus behind their doors. But there had been no sign of Mala.

"There will be time for that later," Perla said. "Finish getting your beauty paint and hair done. We'll see you soon."

They hugged again, and Ariel watched Perla go. She swam a little straighter, sure she could do this because her sisters were with her.

After what felt like a lifetime, Ariel's auburn locs were pulled up in an elegant bun, with her shell-and-pearl headpiece affixed on it. She glanced at the looking glass and gasped, her hand stuck to her mouth like a starfish. She couldn't believe what she was seeing. The headpiece fit on her head perfectly; the shawl complemented her rich, earthy skin tone. She *looked* like a real Protector, as all her sisters had before her. She turned, eyeing the back of the shawl: the way its coral fibers were woven in a crisscross pattern, pearls here and there.

"All right then, you're simmering like a pot of fish stew in front of that looking glass," Julia teased. She seemed slightly more relaxed now that Ariel was finished getting ready, but Ariel still noticed an air of anxiety about her. "The time is near. Get moving." Ariel gave her housekeeper a hug and thanked the hairdresser before taking one more glance at herself and hurrying out the door.

Music swelled in the entryway as Sebastian conducted a symphony of puffer fish in the sweetest melody. Guests filled the corridor, and Ariel swooned at the way the palace had been transformed. Seaflora woven into swags was pinned to the walls, and woven soft coral had been swathed along the windows and ran along the aisle she would swim for her procession. Glowfish tucked in their orbs sat along the aisle, lighting the way like a moonlit pathway.

She craned for a view of a familiar face or two. The same people usually attended these things: father's dignitaries, his most loyal subjects from all over the kingdom, from seas far across the globe, each clamoring for a chance to kiss the hand of the newest Protector. Today's crowd seemed smaller than she had imagined, but Ariel didn't think much of it.

She spotted a few familiar faces and waved. Donalous the dolphin was one of Father's longtime friends. He was nice, but a bit too chatty. If she got locked into a conversation with him, they'd never start on time. Ariel turned the other way. She spotted Borea, head of the Royal Guard, and Koika, the tiger shark Father entrusted with the royal history. They waved at her from their circle of poised conversation.

Outside, clusters of Carinaeans clung to the gate like barnacles, shouting Ariel's name. Colorful bulbs flew through the spires in a shower of kelp confetti, and Ariel dug her teeth into her knuckle. All this for *her*. She stroked the bead on her wrist and took a deep breath. With her sisters' support, she was going to do her best to be beyond magnificent at being a Protector.

Just outside the gates, outlined by a wreath of shells spotted with glowfish, was the dais where the royal family would sit. But only Caspia and Indira were in their spots so far. Bells chimed as her Father appeared out of nowhere, stress digging into his brow. "Well, don't you look breathtaking?"

Ariel smiled, pushing down her nerves. "Thank you, Father. I think I'm ready."

"Looking sharp, Princess, Sire," Usengu said, rushing by, his fins full of extra glowing orbs to replace several guests accidentally shattered. Father's lips broke into a smile, and he exhaled.

"Oh, and this is for you!" Her father handed her a single stem of water orchid. "For luck! Unless, of course, you already have a fish in your pocket?" He pulled it back playfully.

"I'll take the flower." She laughed. "Thank you."

Her father kissed her cheek. "Get in place. We'll be starting soon." He gazed through the domed glass windows at the stage set beyond the gates. "Your sisters should have been lined up—"

"Five shells ago," Sebastian shouted over his shoulder, his claws waving the music in motion from a raised platform in the middle of the vestibule.

Karina and Perla zipped past. Their arms were painted in ceremonial patterns and colors, artfully drawn to complement the unique, territory-inspired headpieces they wore. Karina's was a collection of glass spires reminiscent of the icy coral found only in Saithe.

"Keep your head down when they toss the confetti," Perla shouted.

"Getting some in your eye is the worst," Karina added. "Ask me how I know."

"Head down, got it." Ariel flashed her sisters a thumbs-up as they disappeared beyond the grand foyer doors to find their places onstage. She touched the band across her forehead, making sure it was secure. Silver swirls dotted with turquoise streaked her arms. Everyone was in place except for Mala. Ariel tapped her fin. *Where is she?*

Ariel spotted a stern-faced Indira and Caspia swimming in her direction, their arms tightly crossed. *Great.* The crowd was growing restless waiting for the procession to start. Even the clock worm folded his spindly arms in frustration. The puffer fish tunes rose with the high clash of cymbals and a low hum before switching to her marching music. Ariel's neck flashed hot as she gazed back toward Mala's room.

"Are we going to be getting started any time soon, or?" a stout fish with long gray whiskers said. "I have somewhere else to be."

Her father, who still had yet to make his way to the stage, pulled to and fro in conversations with his guards, didn't dignify him with a response.

"Father." Ariel flagged him. "That guest—"

"Can wait," her father snapped. Ariel didn't like to see the guest ignored, and apparently the stout fish didn't either, because once he realized his question had been disregarded, he stormed out and left.

"Leave it to Mala to mess this up and make it all about her," Caspia muttered. "I'd say I'm surprised, but I'm not."

Ariel fidgeted to keep a handle on her nerves.

"Where is Princess Mala?" a guest whispered behind a fin to another guest, close enough for Ariel to hear as she swam off. "Aiming for a reputation like that of her sister, I see."

Tamika? How rude! Mala was never late. Curiosity sloshed in Ariel's insides. "I'm going to go check her room," Ariel said.

"I'll go with you," Indira said. "I have a knack for annoying her into compliance."

They ventured up the stairs and found the door to Mala's room ajar. Ariel swam inside.

"Mala, it's time—" She gasped.

Mala's room had been turned upside down. Her shawl was shredded in pieces; the beads of her headpiece were strewn across the floor. Her looking glass was cracked, and the window to her room had been shattered.

"Ah!" Indira screamed. "She's *gone?*" She moved to the window, surveying the broken glass. Ariel picked up her sister's tattered journal of seaweed. The cover had been ripped off. *She's really not here. But how?*

Ariel blinked, trying to find words to put to the mess before her eyes, then spotted a flattened scroll. She picked it up, her fingers blackening with the fresh squid ink. Her heart sank as her eyes soaked in the words. Terrible words.

Abdicate the Sea Throne
and seat it with a fairer ruler by the Coral Moon
or never see the princess again.

Chapter
5

Four Days Until the Coral Moon

Indira gasped when Ariel showed her the note. She backed away in fear and knocked over some fragile baubles that spilled from the table in Mala's room.

"Stay calm," Ariel said, despite her insides feeling like two jellyfish squished together. "Let's think."

The throne? Who would do such a thing?

"Think? What is there to think about? We have to warn everyone!" Indira said, her fingers clawing at her throat. "Father's throne," she choked out. "I *knew* coming here . . . somewhere so unprotected, without a Resident, and tensions

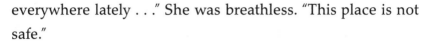
everywhere lately . . ." She was breathless. "This place is not safe."

"You don't think Sea Monsters had anything to do with this?" Ariel asked.

"Who else would it be?" Indira snatched for the note, but Ariel held it firmly in her hands. She wouldn't jump to conclusions. Her sister huffed and rushed out the door. Ariel darted back down to the lower level as fast as her fins would take her, but Indira was much faster and reached the crowded foyer before Ariel could stop her.

"Indira, wait!" She didn't want to alarm everyone. They should pull Father aside and tell him. That seemed wise, right? She spotted her father still making greetings in the foyer. Caspia, Perla, and Karina had found their way back to the stage outside the gates. Ariel had just started toward them when Indira's voice sliced through the pre-ceremony revelry.

"Father! Mala . . . her room," Indira shouted at no one in particular, and thus at everyone. "She's been taken by some- one who wants your throne!"

The crowd's eyes darted around the room in crinkled curiosity. Sebastian's band stopped, and the only thing that could be heard was the swish of water. Not a fish spoke. For a moment the entire ocean seemed to still.

"What is this?" Her father swam to meet them, and Ariel handed him the note.

"We found this in Mala's room just now." Ariel offered a timid smile to the audience, trying to stave off the growing chaos. But inside all she could see was Mala's ripped shawl and the jagged glass of her broken window. She hugged herself, fighting off the urge to scream.

Calm. She had to remain calm. She was to be their Protector. She couldn't freak out.

Father's brow deepened, eyes widening as he read the words over and over again. Finally he said, "Stay here, all of you. I'm going to check the premises. Sebastian, resume the music. Guards!"

The world tilted on its axis as Ariel watched her father storm off, his guards with him. As soon as they cleared the upper level, chaos erupted in a cloud of sea dust.

"The princess has been kidnapped!" Shouts rang out from the crowd. "Sea Monsters are after the crown! Danger! Run!" Guests swam in every direction, shoving each other to get through the clogged funnel of the gate.

"Come on, a light tune now. Something soothing," Sebastian urged the puffer fish, but despite his attempt to appear normal among the storm of fearful guests, the crab's expression was more concerned than usual.

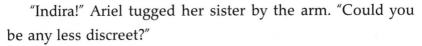

"Indira!" Ariel tugged her sister by the arm. "Could you be any less discreet?"

The rest of her sisters swam back inside, right toward them, curious over the ruckus.

"Indira, talk to me. What did you see?" Caspia shook Indira by the shoulders.

"Her room!" Indira stared into the distance, trembling. "It—it was empty and stuff was everywhere. It looked like she had been attacked!"

Indira fainted into Caspia's arms; Caspia began wailing. Karina had backed into a corner, curled in on herself as if she'd seen a ghost. Perla clung to Ariel's side, speechless, her fins rigid in shock.

"You!" Caspia pointed a judging finger at Karina. "You probably left the gates open yesterday when we returned from the memorial, and someone snuck in! Admit it! Didn't you?" She petted Indira's head, which was still on her lap. "She's so forgetful. All the time."

"Don't you start with me!" Karina fired back, visibly shaken. The fraying peace Ariel had brokered with her sisters was down to a thread.

"Caspia—" Ariel started, but a guest rushed past her so violently it knocked her aside.

"No, no, I don't want to hear it," Caspia retorted as Ariel

steadied herself. "This is somehow her fault. She's always messing up."

"I'm not listening to you!" Karina shoved past them both, heading toward her room before turning back. "There's a reason Indira is the *only* friend you have, Caspia. Think about that!"

"Karina! Please," Ariel pleaded.

"Don't please *me*. Please *her*!"

"Wh-what happened?" Indira batted her eyes open, coming to. "Wh-what did Karina do?"

"She got Mala *kidnapped* and probably killed with her carelessness!"

Indira gasped before fainting all over again.

"Caspia!" Perla chastised. "I can't stand Karina any more than you can, but you shouldn't say such things!"

The music wore on, and an obedient Sebastian kept darting glances at the upper level, where Father had disappeared with his guards. The guests were full-on fighting to get through the exit. Beyond the glass dome, Ariel could see the gates to the palace buckling against the shove of the crowd. The bickering between her sisters grated her nerves.

"*SILEEENCE!*" The bone walls of the palace shook at her father's voice. Everything and everyone stopped. Worry weighed down his brow, but his next words came out measured and calm. "I've just confirmed with the guards that

Princess Mala is not inside the palace. We won't jump to conclusions until we've had time to search Carinae properly. But for now, the Protector Ceremony for Ariel must be postponed."

The few fish that hadn't wedged themselves out the door bowed to their king.

"Proceed to the exit *calmly*," he said. "Get back to your homes."

Perla dug her nails into Ariel's arm. Ariel's stomach did flips as she watched the crowd disperse, more orderly now that their king had spoken.

"I'm going to go back to Mala's room and look for anything that could help," Ariel told Perla. She couldn't just wait and do nothing, not when her father had confirmed that Mala was gone.

"You're most certainly not!" It was King Triton butting into her and Perla's conversation. "Caspia, Indira, all of you, to your rooms. And do not come out until I've told you the place is clear."

"But, Father, I—" Ariel started.

"To your room!" His voice boomed.

Ariel folded her arms, her frustration boiling over. This was her territory, and that was her sister! She couldn't sit on the sidelines for this. She'd been too young to have done anything when Mother went missing. But she was a whole fifteen years old, and Protector . . . well, almost . . . of her own territory.

"No, Father—"

"Ariel, go to your room or, so help me, I will lock you in there myself!" He turned to his guards, who were hovering nearby, awaiting further instructions. "Find Usengu and meet me in my chambers. I want a full report on the growing tensions I've been hearing of, *now!*"

"Just come on." Perla tugged at Ariel's arm. "No one can get through to him when he's like that."

Ariel bit her lip in determination. Perla was right. But still . . . As the rest of her sisters fled to their rooms in panic, Ariel followed at a slow pace and lingered at her door. Once her sisters were all inside their own quarters, she swam down the corridor to Mala's room. Hers was the only one in that wing of the palace, and it had been barricaded shut and flanked by guards.

Ariel knew that her father and his guards must have checked Mala's room, but she doubted that, in their hurry, they had actually taken the time to inspect it for any clues. Everyone seemed ready to believe that a Sea Monster was to blame, but what if there was something left inside that could give them a real answer? Ariel had to find out for herself.

"Princess, please go back to your room," one of the guards

said once they saw her approach. Ariel gave them what she hoped was a charming smile.

"I'm on orders from Fath—the king to check if any of our personal things are in Mala's room as a precaution. You see, we slept over together last night there, and the king doesn't want any of our items to get mixed up with potential evidence."

Not true. We slept in my room, but the guard won't know that detail, will he?

The swordfish considered her a moment before moving aside to let her through. Ariel hurried past him.

Seeing the room again wasn't any easier. The shell frame of Mala's bed and its jellyfish cushion were in a heap on the floor as if they had been torn in half with sheer strength. Shattered glass and a pile of her sister's things were overturned like trash on the floor. Ariel shuddered and quickly sifted through all the debris. She rummaged through the wreckage until her arms ached. She wasn't sure exactly what she was looking for, other than some clearer picture of what had happened. How had her things ended up broken and scattered everywhere? Had she fought off her kidnapper? Why hadn't they heard anything?

Ariel's head hurt with questions that made it feel like the walls were closing in. This wasn't happening. It wasn't. *It had.* She moved to the window, which was lined with broken glass, sharp and triangular like a mouth of shark teeth. Ariel picked at the pieces of glass that were barely hanging on. *They must have left through here.* She stuck her head ever so carefully through the window, watching her scales on the glass. Something green flickered in the sunlight on the ocean floor below. She squeezed herself all the way through. The green something was a shred of sea kelp rolled up like parchment.

She unrolled the leaf and gasped. It was a note, smudged with small marks Ariel couldn't recognize, hastily written in slanted script.

What could have saved Mother
could save me, too.

Ariel stared at the words in shock. She recognized the handwriting from when she had practiced her letters as a fry. Mala.

How would Mala have known to leave a note? Had she been able to anticipate her kidnapper before they arrived? And if she had known she was about to be taken, why not write something more helpful instead of a cryptic message about their mother?

"Princess, are you almost finished?" the guard called from

the other side of the door. Ariel swam back inside through the window and hurried to leave the room.

"Thank you, I'm all done," she told the guard, hoping they wouldn't question her. She clenched the kelp tight in her fist and hurried toward King Triton's lair.

She had to tell her father about what she had found. Mala had left them a clue, as vague as it was, and it could be the key to finding her.

"Ariel? What are you doing out of your room?" It was Karina, in front of her own room, her mollusk handbag stuffed to the brim.

"I'm going to see Father," Ariel said, but she stopped, brows furrowing at Karina's luggage. "Wait, what are you doing? Where are you going?"

"*Shhh.*" Karina darted a glance around and pulled them both into her room. "I—I need to get back home."

"Home?" *With us is your home,* Ariel wanted to say. But her sisters hadn't acted like they believed that in some time. Sometimes it felt like Ariel was the only one holding on to the warm, fuzzy feeling of home from her childhood. The way they'd swim around the reef garden in the afternoons when she was really small, and laughter filled their walls. The memories were faint whispers, but she could still hear them if she really listened. And they stirred a warmth in her

Ariel longed to feel again, she realized. She didn't want to just find Mala. She wanted *them* to find Mala, together.

Ariel unrolled the kelp. "Please don't go. Look what I found outside of Mala's room. I want to take it to Father and have him let me help. This is my sea—"

"Father's out right now with the guards. He's already formed a search party." Karina grabbed her wrist tight. "Ariel, give it to him when he returns and leave this alone. Promise me."

"Karina, please—"

"Listen to me, Lula." Karina's nickname for Ariel was her favorite. She said it was what Mother had called her when she was a little fry. Mother had been trying to teach her to say her own name, but all Ariel could manage was "lula." And it stuck.

"If what that kelp says is true, Mala is in serious danger. I don't want . . ." She tucked hair behind Ariel's ear. *"Mother* wouldn't want anything to happen to you. Please. Give that to Father when he returns, and then go back to his palace where it is safe."

"Leave?" Ariel asked indignantly. "But I just got here! I'm to be their Protector! Like all of you are. I have a job to do, too."

"Read that kelp again, Lula. Mala is in serious danger. Father isn't going to let any of us get involved."

"But I am the one who found this clue," Ariel said, gripping tightly to the note in her hand. "It was the first place I looked. Father didn't catch it."

"You think you're smarter than Father?" asked Karina.

"That's not what I meant. But I do have good ideas."

"Of course you do, but Father's stubborn. He won't see it that way." Karina kissed her forehead. "Listen to me, Lula. Do what I said. I have to go." And with that, Karina was off.

Karina's grave expression sent a chill down Ariel's spine. She had planned to talk to Father, but he was gone. If that note meant her sister's kidnapping had something to do with their mother, she couldn't waste time. She had no idea when Father would be back, and she wasn't entirely sure he would even listen to her. She had to do something right *then*. Could she get her other sisters to help? Maybe they knew more about her mother's death; maybe the note would make more sense to them.

Ariel turned back and rapped her fist on Indira and Caspia's door. The door swung open and Indira greeted her. Her hair was a tangled mess, as if she'd spent the last several moments trying to literally pull it out.

"What are you doing here? Are you okay?"

"Uh, yes. Sorry," Ariel said. "Can I come in?"

"You should be in your room, like Father said, you know." Indira gave her the side-eye but opened the door wider. A good sign. Inside, Ariel found Caspia cleaning. She did that when she was nervous.

Ariel squeezed the note in her fist. *Not yet.* She had to be sure they were on the same page she was before she revealed her blatant defiance.

"You feeling better?" she asked Indira.

"I'm just so worried. Father will sort it out, though. He said some Carinaean Sea Monster is likely behind it," Indira said.

But how does he know that? The note didn't mention anything about Sea Monsters. Why would he think that?

"Have you all ever had issues with the Sea Monsters in your territories before?" Ariel asked.

"Are you serious?" Caspia said to her before turning to Indira. "Is she serious?"

Ariel hated when they treated her that way. Like she knew nothing because all this Protector business was newer to her. But she swallowed her frustration and thought of Mala. She wouldn't pick a fight with them over it. Not now.

"Of course we have. In Apneic, the last several weeks have been a nightmare, with chimaeras flooding the river-beds with their scales. And it's like no matter how many times I hold court with them to tell them scales can only be shed in the designated areas, they just railroad over me, going on about the drainage in those areas being clogged." Caspia scoffed in frustration.

"Is there a way to fix the drainage issue *and* keep the scale shedding to a restricted area? Maybe the Resident could tell them you're working on not just your rules, but their concerns as well?" Ariel asked. That seemed . . . reasonable? Wasn't that the point of having a Resident? To liaise between them and help keep the peace? "Usengu always says—"

"Not even a Protector yet and she's got all the solutions, Caspia, can you believe it?" Indira folded her arms.

"Please, I'm just trying to help," Ariel shot back before she could pull it back. "I'm just trying to help."

"And you're naive," Indira snapped.

Ariel sighed. "Look, I don't want to fight. I want to find Mala." She hadn't meant for the truth to slip out. But she was tired of the back-and-forth.

"What do you mean, *find*?" Caspia's brows kissed.

Ariel showed them the kelp. "Look. Does this make any sense to you? I think it is from Mala, and I'm trying to figure out what it means."

They read it and gasped. Indira's eyes shimmered as she shook her head in disbelief.

Silence.

"If you are right and Mala wrote this, then this is dangerous." Indira could hardly meet Ariel's eyes.

"I know, but—"

"Father should sort this kind of thing out. You have to

give him that." Caspia snatched at the kelp, but Ariel was faster. "Give it to me!" her sister yelled, but the strain in her voice was all fear, not anger. She was scared. They were all scared. Getting them to help wasn't going to work; they were too shaken. "I mean it, Ariel!" Caspia folded her arms, and the two of them glowered at her.

This was a mistake.

"Tell him!"

"Or we will!"

"Of course I'm going to tell him! He's not here right now. What do you suggest? We do nothing?"

"Go wait in his room right this minute, Ariel, and give him that the moment he gets back." They urged her to the door, and she could tell her time of being welcome in their room had come to an end. The door closed in her face before she could respond.

They were impossible. But there was one sister Ariel knew she could count on. She rushed to Perla's room, pleasantly surprised to find her door unlocked.

"Oh, my goodness! I'm so worried," Perla said, pulling her into a hug. "I came looking for you to see how you're doing. Where are you coming from? Was there word from Father or anyone?"

"No, but look what I found outside Mala's room." She

handed her the kelp, and Perla's brows crinkled. Ariel explained how she'd found it and the endless questions she had about what it could mean. "It didn't seem to make much sense to Indira or Caspia, either. But it seems to suggest that looking into Mother's death is how we figure out how to help Mala."

Perla read it again, then paced. "Did you tell Father?"

"He's not here right now. I was thinking we could look into it . . . ourselves?"

"You're kidding. Tell me you're kidding, Ari."

Ariel turned to her sister. Could she understand? "I should be assisting with the investigation. The high-sun side of Carinae is my soon-to-be territory. I was going to *ask* Father to let me help, truly. But he isn't here right now, and we can't do nothing."

Perla chewed her lip, discomfort denting her worn expression. She wasn't quite sold on Ariel's plan just yet, but it appeared she was considering it. "You make a good point."

"If I do nothing but let my daddy fix it, what does that make me look like?" Ariel would show him how resourceful she could be. She slipped out of her shawl. "Help me with the headpiece." Her mind was made up. She was doing this with or without Perla.

"Ariel—"

"Perla!"

Perla sighed but swam over to help Ariel disconnect the pearl crown from her head. "What are we doing?"

We. Ariel had known Perla would eventually agree to help her.

"We're going to investigate, starting with the only place on this side of Carinae that has anything to do with Mother."

Chapter 6

Four Days Until the Coral Moon

With Father off the premises with most of his guards, sneaking out of the castle would be easy. Mother's memorial near the Protector palace had the closest connection to her death of anywhere in the area, so Ariel decided that's where they would head first to see if Mala had left them any more clues, or if something there sparked some clarity on what the note could mean.

"Come on, this way." She and Perla eased down the corridor and into the foyer that had rung with revelry just moments earlier. Garlands, once strung along the windows, had been strewn across the floor in everyone's haste to get out. The seafloor was a collection of dirtied confetti, shattered glass, and broken shells. But Ariel fixed her gaze straight ahead and pulled Perla along toward the exit.

"Princess," someone shouted after her, "is it true the king is being asked to abdicate?"

But Ariel ignored the few lingering Carinaean seafolk as they flung questions about this whole mess in her direction.

She tucked her head and swam through them. "Don't make eye contact. Head down." Perla's grip tightened on her hand.

Guilt twisted in her stomach. She should have answers for them. She should be helping them. But figuring out what had happened to Mala was the best help she could give at that moment. For everyone.

On their way out, Ariel spotted Julia pacing back and forth in the corridor. The housekeeper looked paler than usual, as if she was about to be sick. Ariel thought that Julia would tell them to go back to their rooms when she spotted them, but to her surprise, Julia's eyes only widened and she rushed in the other direction.

Together, Ariel and Perla rushed out of the castle to the exact spot where they'd been the evening before. The gate was latched and the dirt was still as they left it, undisturbed.

"Father and his guards haven't searched this area at all!" Ariel said in disbelief.

Perla shrugged. "Good thing we're checking it out, I guess."

"Hmm. Look around for any other signs of Mala coming through here, or something that will help us better understand her note." Ariel pulled at the swaying seaweed cluttered around the base of the statue, glancing underneath the roots for a dropped earring or ripped piece of shawl—some sign of her sister trying to get away from her captor or leaving them more bread crumbs.

But after several moments, nothing turned up, so she widened her search zone, moving outside the gate, farther from the memorial. Perla went in the opposite direction to cover more ground. Ariel combed the seabed, overturning stones and moving brush that had sunk to the floor from the world above until her arms ached. She was just about to give up when a cloud of zooplankton drifted by in a swish.

"Excuse me!" Ariel rushed after them. "Have you seen a mermaid with long dark hair come this way?"

The tiniest among them halted his crew. "You're asking us?"

"Yes, yes," Ariel said, a little confused by their hesitation. "If that's all right?"

He threw up his hands in surrender. "We don't want any trouble."

She furrowed her brow. "Trouble? Why would—"

"We heard the king was collecting seafolk to lock in that dungeon of his. And he feeds them to his daughters!" He put more space between them.

"What?" Ariel shook her head, certain her ears were deceiving her. "No! Where did you hear this?"

"A buddy of mine told me. A buddy of his told him. All kinds of things going around these days."

This was preposterous! Had any of her sisters heard this? Father would never. Sure, he was stubborn with a short fuse, and he'd been detached for years, but locking up merfolk and sea creatures? Eating them? She could have laughed, it was so ridiculous.

"I assure you, the king is not collecting anyone. And I have no interest in hurting you or anything of the sort," Ariel said. "Really, sir, I'm just trying to find my sister. I'm sorry if I've alarmed you."

His expression of grave concern melted into sheer confusion.

"Your sister, you say?"

Ariel nodded.

Chatter broke out among the group of zooplankton, their heads shaking.

"Oh, no, miss, I'm sorry to say we have not seen anyone."

Ariel sighed. "Thank you. Please do keep an eye out, and if you see anything unusual, please come find me." She pointed at the palace. "Here. I—I'm Ariel. I'm to be Carinae's Protector. And you are?"

His tiny little mouth twisted, still perplexed by her, a princess, wanting to know his name. "Gus. We're all Gus," he finally said. The collection of heads nodded behind him.

"Nice to meet you, Gus . . . ses?"

The original Gus bowed his head in salute just as a ripple in the ocean took them. And Ariel could have sworn she heard them mutter, "Thanks for not eating us."

What has gotten into folks?

"Any luck?" It was Perla, holding a net tangled with a bunch of debris. Broken shiny glass, barbs, a few shiny hooks, and other speckled curiosities were caught in the fibers of the net.

"None," Ariel said. "What's all this?"

"Junk." Perla dropped the pile, and it fluttered to the ground. "But look here." She'd pulled out a tuft of hair tangled in the net. "I think it's Mala's."

Ariel took the hair. It certainly looked like her sister's, but it could have belonged to any mermaid with dark hair. It could also have fallen out at any time when she'd visited before. Could it be coincidence? She tapped her lip and glanced at the heap her sister had been holding, now in a pile on the seafloor. *There could be more clues in there.*

"Let me see that." Ariel sifted through the net, detaching

things that had been caught in its ropes, careful to set aside each one so she could inspect it more closely. A shard of broken glass gleamed pink.

Is that . . . Ariel examined it closer, picking at it with her nail, and bits of it came off. *Paint?* Mala had planned to wear pink body paint for the ceremony, inspired by the vividly colorful foliage in Chaine.

Ariel picked through the net, sifting for a better understanding of how Mala's body paint could have ended up on those bits of glass. It felt like trying to find treasure in sinking sand. One end of the net, she realized, had been ripped to shreds. As if it had been hooked on something but forcibly pulled away. Her tongue poked her cheek. What did that mean? Could Mala have tried to pull at the net to claw herself away from them, and it broke? Ariel wasn't sure. The hair. The paint. She had to have come this way, at least, right? *Gosh, it would be so much easier searching if I had a better grasp on the territory.* The books she had studied over the years had shown her much, but there was something to be said about getting to know a place by exploring it firsthand. And she didn't know that side of Carinae like that. Not yet.

Perla led her to a spot a whole two whalebones away, near a bed of rainbow-colored reef. "I found it here."

Ariel considered the area, gazing between the direction they'd come and where the path before them led. Its scenery was entirely unfamiliar to Ariel. It wasn't the way to the Carinaean palace, the way home, or even the way to the memorial. It was barren, with darker, deep waters and sparser foliage. If she had seen a picture of it, she wouldn't even have known it was on the high-sun side of Carinae. With as beautiful as her territory was, she couldn't imagine any of its seafolk choosing to live there. Perhaps that's why it was so desolate.

The light shifted, and a low rumble echoed in the distance. Ariel gazed up at the clouds rolling in in the world above them. Their father would likely be back soon, and she needed to tell him what she had found. Ariel was turning to tell Perla they needed to head back when her fin hit a sign staked in the ground.

SEA MONSTERS
RESTRICTED ACCESS

The realization stilled her. This area was where Carinaean Sea Monsters lived. The weight of it tugged at her shoulders for a reason she wasn't quite sure how to put into words. The feeling confused her. On the one hand, the Treaty suggested— and Father would have her believe—that keeping creatures designated Sea Monsters restricted to their territories kept the whole sea safer. He seemed convinced, according to her sisters, that someone from this area was behind Mala's kidnapping and the attempt to take his throne. Still, she didn't like the assumption of who was behind this.

"We should go back," Ariel said. "But I'd like to talk to someone from here. Perhaps the Resident, once they're assigned."

"Oh, you'll talk to them plenty." Perla shuddered.

Ariel shrugged her sister off. That was one point she and her sisters, all but Mala, had never agreed on. They'd all been spooked by Father's wariness of Sea Monsters and the outside world. But that felt a bit suffocating to Ariel. The others always wrote it off as a symptom of having been so young when Mother died. They thought she just didn't get the big deal of how dangerous the ocean was, and her family saw Sea Monsters as the embodiment of that danger. While as far as Ariel knew Sea Monsters were not responsible for her mother's death, the tragedy had seemed to make everyone less trusting.

"I mean . . . the Treaty is clear," Perla said, snatching Ariel from her brooding. "'A monster and a mermaid would protect each of the seven seas, forbidden to love, forbidden to flee.'"

The whole thing seemed pretty tragic on the Sea Monsters' side of things. Sure, the Treaty meant those designated as Sea Monsters had direct representation under her Father's reign through a Resident. But it also meant that when anything went wrong, they got blamed for it and were expected to have answers.

Ariel was about to respond to her sister when something white flashed.

"Shh!" Ariel slowed her pace. They slunk back in the shadows and watched as a plump young white fish with blue stripes sifted between strands of seaweed, overturning leaves on the ground. Could he have seen something? Could he be looking for Mala, too?

"I'm going to talk to him," Ariel said.

Perl's nails dug into her arm. "No! You don't even know if he's dangerous!"

"What?" She shook her sister's grip off, brow furrowed. "He's tiny."

"He's small, but that doesn't mean anything. Those fins could be poisonous."

Ariel rolled her eyes. "Fine, you stay here. I'll yell if I need help."

"Ariel!"

But she was long gone and on the fish's tail. As he overturned rock after rock, Ariel noticed his fins were shaking.

"Um, hi there," Ariel said.

The little fish yelped before diving under a nestle of sea brush he'd just looked beneath. Despite his effort to fully hide himself, his tail stuck out the back end, shaking more violently.

"I'm sorry!" Ariel squeezed her hands in regret. "I didn't mean to scare you."

"No, no, don't come any closer," he pleaded. "P-please."

Gosh, she felt bad. Ariel put some space between them to give him a moment to see she wasn't a threat. She flashed a look at Perla—a whole mermaid, five times his size and yet also terrified, shielding herself behind a stand of kelp. The irony was laughable.

"I'm Ariel," she tried.

The whole nest of plants he hid in shook.

"I won't hurt you, I promise." She set down the net Perla had found with the tuft of hair and broken glass. She held up her hands in surrender. "I don't have anything to harm you."

He peeped his head out a little, eyeing her up and down.

"I was just out looking around for something, and, well, you seemed like you were looking for things, too. I just thought I'd say hi."

"Hi." The fish stuck his whole head out, darting a glance in every direction before settling his gaze on Ariel. His fins shook less. It wasn't much, but she took it, shrugging and offering a smile, careful to respect the hefty distance between them. "I—I don't want any trouble. Just searching for something. B-but if you prefer I go, I—I can."

"Of course not. You were here before us," Ariel said. "What are you looking for? Maybe I've seen it."

"I—I, um. Well, I was trying to find a doheckler."

"A what?" Ariel hadn't heard of such a thing in her life.

"Maybe I'm saying it wrong. My bird friend gave it to me, saying it would be helpful to find shiny treasure."

A fish who keeps company with birds? How thrilling!

"Only I dropped it somewhere. Here, I thought." He tapped his mouth.

"I don't have the slightest clue what that is. I'm sorry you can't find it," said Ariel. "How long have you been looking?"

His gaze fell. "Um, f-four days, I think."

Ariel bit her lip. Anything he'd dropped had likely been pushed around by the current by now. What to do? She waved Perla over. Perla seemed to have realized the young fish was not a threat. She came out of her hiding place and swam up beside them, offering a timid wave.

"This is my sister Perla," Ariel said. "We didn't catch your name."

"Flounder."

"Nice to meet you, Flounder," Perla said, her shoulders sinking a bit.

He narrowed his eyes. "Wait, are you . . ." He gasped and backed away. "I'm sorry, Your Highness. You're the king's daughters!" He squeezed his head between his fins and spun in a circle, only further winding up his panic. "I'm talking to the king's daughters! I—I should bow or . . ." He dipped down low in his best fishly bow. "Forgive me, please."

"Oh, no, please," Ariel said. "No need for any of that. By the way, have you seen any mermaids come this way?"

Flounder tapped his head. Then he pointed in the direction of the desolate waters Ariel had been fretting about earlier. "I did see a Sea Monster go that way."

"I *knew* it," her sister muttered. "I told you, sis."

Ariel still wasn't convinced.

Flounder's face scrunched in confusion. "I've met a whole host of Sea Monsters from the seas I've traveled. I've been in High Sun for moons. The water this time of year is at its clearest, and all kinds of flora in this sea *only* bloom now. I just love it. Not to mention all the algae this way. There are more than forty different kinds." He grabbed his tummy. "I've been to each of the seven territories three times, but this one is my favorite to visit this time of year. I was actually planning to make another round of visits to each territory soon, but then I lost my thing."

"You know a lot about the area," Ariel said.

His mouth pushed sideways in a bashful smile. "Gee, thanks."

He probably knows a lot from his travels, Ariel thought. Could he help them?

But Flounder was timid, shy, and absolutely terrified of his own shadow. Finding a missing mermaid wasn't something he'd likely be up for. Maybe she could ease him into it. Make him feel safe.

"I need to know more about this territory and its creatures. Would you be open to helping me . . . with information, I mean? Nothing dangerous. You could stay at the Protector's palace. We could look into whether we have any do-hay-clurs."

Perla side-eyed her and Ariel gulped before painting on a smile.

"Come to court?" Flounder's big eyes doubled in size. "Me, come to court?"

"Yes!"

"I—I don't know," he said. "It sounds crowded and—"

"Nope, you can have a room to yourself."

"This is not a good idea. How exactly are you going to pull this off?" Perla muttered through her teeth. Ariel ignored her. The fish tapped his head again, considering.

"There's food," Ariel went on. "So much food! Algaecakes and crustaloaves. The royal kitchens can drum up anything you like."

"Um . . ." His lips puckered and he bonked himself on the head again. His eyes darted between them. "It *has* been a while since I've had a good bite."

Ariel beamed in anticipation.

"And, well . . ." He tapped his face with his fin. "I can leave whenever I want?"

"Absolutely," Ariel promised.

"Um, o-okay. I—I can help you."

Ariel shook his fin, studying him. What would Father make of him helping? Would he be open to it? It seemed like such a good idea to her. They really could use his help. Father *had* to be able to see that she was taking this Protector role seriously. She swam off, leading the way back to the palace. Despite not having found anything super helpful on their investigation, she was sure landing Flounder's help was a win.

Chapter 7

Four Days Until the Coral Moon

Flounder swam behind them timidly, firing off questions the entire way back to the palace about what exactly they'd been doing with their time in High Sun, to which Perla bit her tongue. Fortunately. Ariel answered him, as honestly as she could without tipping him off that they were looking for her sister.

"What were you thinking, bringing him along?" Perla said under her breath as Flounder fell farther behind, still peering around just in case he spotted the shiny knob of his doheckler.

"I'm thinking he'll know more about this territory than

we ever could, since he's been traveling it for moons," Ariel whispered back. "Did you hear how he spouted off stuff about the area?"

"Yeah, but he's terrified of his own shadow."

"And? He's safe with us."

"Is he, though, Ariel?" Her sister dug her nails into her arm. "Are we even safe?"

Ariel frowned at her. "Don't talk like that. We're going to find out who took Mala and get her back." She wouldn't believe anything different.

"Everything okay?" Flounder asked, trailing along behind them. Ariel flashed him a nervous smile.

"Everything's great!" she said, with a little too much enthusiasm, but Flounder had stopped paying attention. He swam ahead of them, his eyes focused on something in front of him.

"Have you seen this?" Flounder waved his fins as if he were waxing a glass wall. "There's a seal around the palace." He rippled the water with his fin, and a veil shimmered orange.

"There is?" Ariel asked.

Father had Safety Seals around their castle back home and her sisters' palaces in their territories. It was an invisible barrier, like a giant bubble. He'd infused it with his trident so that only those with permission could cross. Ariel had seen a dumbo octopus try to fight the seal once. His lips swelled to twice their original size and he sank to the seabed under their weight, stuck there until the guards took him away. But they'd just gotten to High Sun. How was there one there already? Had Father put it up before they arrived?

"Can you tell how long it's been here?" Ariel asked him.

Flounder pursed his lips. "Well, it looks like it's been here for a long time. But what's more strange," Flounder went on, "is that all the territory palaces have these, but they shimmer blue when you swim to them. This one's orange, open, like it's not working. It's been broken or something. Watch . . ." He swam forward and shoved through the seal. Ariel gasped. That shouldn't work. Anyone could get through.

A crime took place within the palace—my sister kidnapped. And the security seal around the palace to ensure only those invited to the ceremony could get through is broken?

She tapped her lip, a shiver running up her arm as the pieces of a puzzle she was trying desperately to solve sifted between her fingers like sand.

Was the broken seal connected to Mala's disappearance? What else made sense? Whoever took Mala would have needed to get in and out. If the seal had randomly malfunctioned, and Father knew, he'd have someone out fixing it immediately. This stank of sabotage.

Perla clutched the strand of shells dangling at her neck. "Who could break a Safety Seal by the king?"

"Hmm. Well, the king, of course. And Residents have the ability to fiddle with the seals, in case they need to bring someone through to meet with Usengu or something. The king gave them that along with the gifts he bestowed at their commissioning."

"Oh, right," Ariel said. *I hadn't considered that.* She vaguely recalled a mention of that during her studies. Residents were chosen from within their own territories, among their own seafolk. Each Resident had to pass Father's inspection. But once he'd deemed them trustworthy, he gave each Resident a gift, some special ability, as a token of good faith and gratitude. But her studies hadn't covered much more than that about Sea Monsters.

Residents were the handful of Sea Monsters Father trusted. She'd watched an induction ceremony with one once for Mala's territory. The whole kingdom was frightened when they'd heard Ieka the Notorious—called such because his family were ravenous hunters who feasted on all manner of sea creatures and mermaids—was to be deemed Resident in Chaine. But he swore he'd never had the appetite his parents had and much preferred a sea plant diet. He passed all of King Triton's tests. So he was made Resident. Ariel couldn't recall what gift her father had given him. She had been so small; she remembered being wrapped around Tamika's arm, watching it all. Flounder was right—besides the king himself,

Residents were the only others who could fiddle with the Safety Seal.

Does that mean . . . She cupped her mouth in disbelief. *It must.* Whoever had broken the seal had taken, or aided in taking, Mala? She wrapped her arms around herself. Residents were *trusted*. It didn't make sense. She glared at the broken orange seal. And yet . . . it was the *only* thing that made sense. There were six Residents. And none of them had attended the ceremony, Usengu'd said. They were needed in their territories to keep an eye on things, but what if one had shown up anyways? Ariel's stomach sloshed with nerves. It looked like those six were the likeliest suspects.

Ariel met her sister's eyes, which were pinched and full to the brim with worry. She could tell her sister was thinking the same thing.

The knot in Ariel's chest tightened.

"This is good," she said to Perla. "We're narrowing things down."

"What are we narrowing down?" Flounder had crept up behind her.

Ariel stilled her shaky hands and blew out a breath. Calm. She had to remain calm.

"Oh, I—I meant what could have happened to the seal." That was sort of true. "Let's get inside." She pointed at the palace. Flounder considered her for a moment and nodded.

Together they swam into the palace, careful to make sure that no guards spotted them. Perla whispered to Ariel that she would check and see if their father had returned yet before darting ahead of them. As they passed the empty foyer where Ariel's Protector Ceremony had almost taken place, Flounder looked down nervously at the broken decorations only half cleaned up from the day's earlier events. Ariel just smiled reassuringly.

"So! The Residents," Ariel said quickly once they had reached her quarters. She pulled out squid ink and a strip of tarp and wrote down all six territories with Residents.

> PITON SEA
>
> FRACUS SEA
>
> SAITHE SEA
>
> APNEIC SEA
>
> BRINEDIVE SEA
>
> CHAINE SEA

"What has you so concerned about who broke the Safety Seal?" asked Flounder.

"Uh—" Ariel's eyes darted to avoid his curious gaze. "Oh, um, I'm just thinking that maybe whoever broke the seal was trying to get to the castle to have an audience with Father or Usengu. It could have been something important." She bit her lip, hoping he didn't sense her tentative tone. In truth, if a Resident was behind Mala's kidnapping—*if*, and she certainly hoped they weren't—she wanted to know all she could about where they were and what they could do so she understood what she and her family were potentially up against. "Do you know the Residents' names and sea designations?" Ariel had studied the Residents briefly in sea history, but it had been a while. Her teachers rarely covered topics concerning Sea Monsters, and while she still remembered some information, Flounder's knowledge would be helpful.

He considered her a moment before peering more closely at the names. "Of course I do. I've seen most of them in passing on my travels. And I've heard plenty of stories about all of them." His fins stroked the tarp, and Ariel filled in the ones she remember right away.

"Callyne is Resident in Piton Sea," she said.

"Right. When she was sworn in, the King gave her the ability to hear really low sounds anywhere in the ocean. So she can hear threats coming from far away. And Mangus is Resident in Brinedive Sea. I don't actually know what gift the king bestowed on him."

"It's that he can create an underwater vortex." Ariel scribbled furiously, updating their suspect board. She remembered hearing about the Brinedive Resident's powers from her sister Indira. "And here." She tapped her chin. "I think . . . no, Brutus died and his son took over. So that means Roine is Resident in Apneic, right?"

"Yes, that's correct." Flounder and she went on until each of the Residents was listed, along with the bestowed gifts they could remember. Between her and Flounder, they could recall only five out of the six Residents' abilities.

PITON SEA–CALLYNE
Can hear really low sounds

ERACUS SEA–SILIUS
Unknown gift

SAITHE SEA–TOLUM
Cannot lie

APNEIC SEA–ROINE
Can swell his body to double its size

BRINEDIVE SEA–MANGUS
Can create an underwater vortex

CHAINE SEA–IEKA
Can cause paralysis

Flounder held his tummy. "Not to interrupt our busy work, but did you say they had algaecakes?"

Ariel looked up from the tarp. How could she have been so rude?

"Yes! I'm so sorry," she said. The kitchens had prepared an entire feast for the ceremony. "Let me go see what I can grab. I'll be right back."

Ariel swung the door open and bumped square into Perla.

Perla pushed her back inside and shut the door. "Ariel. Father, he—" She glanced at Flounder and bit her tongue.

"Yeah?" Ariel grabbed her sister by the shoulders, panic wriggling through her like an eel as she ushered Perla into a corner away from Flounder so he wouldn't be able to hear what she was about to say. Had something else happened? Did they have bad news about Mala? "What is it?"

"Father's *furious* Karina left without telling anyone," Perla whispered. "He said we're all returning to his castle right now. He and his guards will finish the investigation themselves. H-he said he is sure some Carinaean Sea Monster is behind it. He's planning to mandate a curfew territory-wide and have his guards comb through the whole place, border to border, and interrogate everyone."

He's wrong, Ariel thought. From her vantage point, the broken seal meant it looked to be a Resident. Not someone in High Sun. Unless the Resident had help, but why would someone in Carinae be working with someone from another territory?

"Interrogation?" Flounder swam over to them. "A Sea Monster is behind what? Does this have to do with the stuff people have been saying about the king?" His voice was measured and even, but his every scale was trembling.

The rumors, he means. Ariel sighed. She wanted to go talk to her father about the clues she had found surrounding Mala's disappearance immediately, but she also knew that if she really wanted Flounder's help, she needed to be honest with him.

"This isn't some research project," Ariel admitted, indicating the tarp. "It's a suspect list. Someone kidnapped my sister this afternoon from my Protector Ceremony, demanding my father give up the throne or we will never see her again." Her voice broke, but she cleared her throat. "And I'm trying to find out who took her and where she could have gone. The clock is ticking. The longer she is gone, the less chance we have of finding her . . . alive."

Flounder's jaw fell open. "An investigation? With, like, a—a real criminal a-and suspects? Th-that's dangerous!"

"Yes, but can't you see that I have to do something?" Ariel put on her best winning smile. "And you're so smart that I thought you might be able to help me."

"I mean, I know a thing or two." His lips pushed sideways

bashfully. "But I could *never* find a suspect o-of a—a crime."

"You're brilliant, Flounder." She petted his head affectionately, and he grinned. "I'm sure you could do that and more."

Flounder closed his mouth, considering what Ariel had said. "You're too nice to say all that about me. I'm on my own all the time b-because sometimes I think I'm not good at anything at all. Never made any friends. That's the real reason I travel so much. To keep from feeling all down about it, I just keep moving."

Ariel let the silence hang a moment. He was lonely. She knew what that was like.

"I'm also sorry for not telling you the full story," she said. "But, Flounder, you're not alone anymore. You don't have to be. You can stay with me. We can make a new home, as friends, here."

He lifted his sullen posture to meet her eyes. "Y-you'd be okay with that?"

"Of course," she urged. "Now, we must talk to my father. When we get back, we can have some algaecakes and figure out what room you can stay in."

Ariel dragged along Flounder, who was terrified of being introduced to the king. She was hardly through the vestibule when her father caught sight of them.

"Father!" She grabbed Flounder by the fin and rushed to meet him.

"Ariel, you should be packing," he said, the lines on his face deepening. "We're leaving at first light."

She cleared her throat, ignoring her stomach doing flips. "Father, since I should be Protector by now, I thought long and hard about it, and I'm staying here in High Sun. I've already managed to figure out that—"

"Who is—"

"Flounder, my new friend." She pulled him forward. He was so nervous she thought he might turn green. "He's more clever than any fish you've ever met. And he knows a lot about the area. He—"

"You brought him in here?" Her father's eyes narrowed. "Got him past my seal?"

"Actually, no. About that—"

"You disobeyed my orders and left your room." He rubbed his temples. "If my hair wasn't already gray, you daughters of mine would make it so."

"Father, please." Ariel eyed Flounder, who was trembling behind her at the king's apparent annoyance. "Say hello." She bit down, hoping he would at least be polite.

He sighed, his expression hardening as he gazed at Flounder. "It's nice to meet you, Fender."

"It's Flounder," Ariel said, her cheeks burning from embarrassment.

"Th-the honor is all mine," Flounder said, bowing his head.

"If you'll excuse us, Fido." Triton pulled her aside. "What could this young fish possibly know about my kingdom that I don't?"

"Father!" She straightened. "That's ridiculous!"

Usengu swam in. "Good evening, Princess, Sire." His expression pinched at Flounder.

"He's with me," Ariel said. She hated the way everyone was so wary of outsiders around here.

"Very well," Usengu said before turning to the king, urgently. "I'm sorry. Forgive me for rudely interrupting. Sire, preparations are ready for the logistics and planning meeting. We have updated reports on sources of tension in the area. We must get a move on it." Usengu leaned in to the king's ear, whispering whatever else he needed to say.

"I'm so sorry about this, Flounder," Ariel told him, but his gaze was glued to the ground in fear of the king.

"Very good," her father said to Usengu. "Bring them in. Anyone suspicious you see. I want to question them myself. I'll be there in a moment."

"But, Father, I found a note in Mala's own hand. And have your guards been to the border? The Safety Seal—"

"*Enough!* Ariel, you will obey me in this or, so help me,

you'll be punished until the next Coral Moon!" His voice boomed, and at her back, Flounder shook harder.

Ariel huffed. "You've given Flounder a fright. Shame on you!" Her father could be insufferable. Frustration burned through her. She snatched Flounder and left her father's audience, fuming. He could be so shortsighted.

She hadn't even gotten to tell him about the seal or Mala's note, not that he would have listened anyway. And this lead or whatever he had on someone in High Sun—was he even on the right track? Ariel and Flounder retreated to her room, where Perla was waiting.

"Well? How'd it go?"

Ariel folded her arms in answer.

"It was a nice thought," Perla said. "Finding Mala ourselves, I mean."

"Oh, our investigation is far from over," Ariel said.

Flounder gulped.

"We're still going to find Mala," Ariel said. "We just have to make sure we keep Father out of our business."

Chapter 8

Three Days Until the Coral Moon

The rest of the day felt like a hazy dream. While Ariel and Perla were confined to their rooms, King Triton and the guards spent the remainder of the afternoon following up on leads and interrogating Carinaeans. Usengu had been sent to the other territories to see what whispers he could glean about Mala's kidnapping. Ariel and her sisters had been pulled out of their beds early the next morning to return to the king's castle, and her tail still ached from the swimming pace her father kept.

Ariel hadn't had a moment to talk to Father and tell him

about the Residents. She had tried to speak to him on the journey home, but every time she brought up the investigation, he told her to leave it to him. Her frustration only grew when, the moment they arrived, the king announced that the castle was on lockdown and that Ariel, her sisters, and Flounder, who Ariel demanded come with them as her guest, were restricted to their rooms.

"What are we, prisoners? In our own home?" Ariel had muttered once the king's back was turned.

"It's for our own safety, sister," Caspia had chastised, coming to their father's defense as usual. "As a Protector, you have to weigh risks, and that's what Father is doing."

Ariel hadn't had the energy to argue back then, but she did manage to whisper to Perla and Flounder that they should sneak out and meet her in her room once they had dropped off their things so that they could help her narrow down their suspect list.

She was relieved to be back among her things. Even with so much of her stuff still in bags being unloaded from the caravan by Julia and the rest of the staff, the familiarity of the walls and objects made her next breath come easier. She could do this. She could find Mala. Another tragedy wouldn't tear them apart . . . more than they were already.

Ariel paced in her room, growing restless as time continued to pass. *Where are they?*

Tap. Tap. She swung the door open, and her heart swelled at seeing Flounder's squishy cheeks.

"Finally!" She looked for Perla, but there was no sign of her in the corridor.

Flounder swam inside, perusing her things. Ariel quickly closed the door behind him after checking to make sure no guards had seen him come in.

"You have a knitter?" Flounder asked.

"What?"

He gestured with his fin to a pointy thing on her shelf. "I heard that's what it's called. My bird friend, Scuttle, told me that's called a knitter, for making fancy things out of colorful seaweed."

Ariel rolled the long silver object between her fingers. She'd found it on the seafloor one evening and had thought it was some sort of digging tool. Though, when she really thought about it, it did seem ill suited for that with its small pointed tip.

Flounder went through the hollowed-out clamshell where the knitter was placed, along with the rest of the surface objects she had collected over the years, and pulled at the tangled mess of what her sisters would have called junk. "You may want to organize this or something." He started sorting through the pieces, and Ariel quickly swept the clamshell away.

"My sisters get on me about it. Father thinks these things are toxic. I prefer to just keep them hidden," Ariel said. *A knitter.* What a curious thing. She turned the stick in her hand again before adding it back to her collection and situating the whole thing behind a shell on her shelf, just so.

"No time to waste. Mala's out there, and we need to help find her." Ariel spread out the tarp with their suspect list on it. Now that Flounder knew what they were really doing with this information, they could get down to the nitty gritty. "So, do you agree? Since Residents are the only ones able to break the seals, Mala's kidnapper has to be one of these six officials."

"Yeah, it's gotta be one of them," Flounder agreed. "I mean, if we're just looking at everyone who is powerful and could mess with the seal, there's Usengu. But, I mean, that doesn't make a lick of sense, given everything I know about him."

Her nose crinkled. *Usengu doesn't have a gift given from Father, does he?* "What do you mean, powerful?"

"Well, Sea Monsters listen to him. He has their ear as Resident Overseer and the king's right hand. They're his seafolk."

Ariel shifted uncomfortably at all the chatter about Usengu. He didn't make sense to add to their suspect list for a lot of reasons. *He's family.* He had also been in the castle the entire time. She'd seen him just moments before Mala went missing, and Father had been in meetings with his guards afterward, which always included Usengu.

"Flounder, everyone in our kingdom is Father's seafolk."

"Sure, technically," said Flounder. "But if that were true, there wouldn't be a Mer–Monster Treaty, would there?"

She couldn't argue with that. He was right. Father had made his position on Sea Monsters clear. Requests from the Sea Monster communities seemed to pile up more than others' did; her father was obviously in no hurry to meet their needs. No wonder they were upset. She'd heard rumors of anger and tension among seafolk, but King Triton always kept the details of those things in closed meetings.

"How do people feel about my father where you've traveled?" Ariel asked Flounder.

Flounder's gaze met the floor.

"You can tell me," Ariel encouraged. "It stays between us, I promise."

"W-well, I mean, in a lot of places Usengu is admired more than the king, to be honest." His eyes shifted nervously, as if just saying that out loud were treason. "B-because he's a voice for the Sea Monsters. He listens to them. They're not . . . I don't know . . . *beasts* to him. Even for someone like me, who isn't a Sea Monster, without much of a voice in the sea . . . Usengu is sort of . . . inspiring, you know?"

Her father had used the term *beast* loosely more than once to describe Sea Monsters, to impress upon Ariel and her sisters that they were scary.

"I won't rule that way," Ariel promised. As Protector, she wouldn't go for that. She'd make sure their needs were met. They were seafolk, like everyone else. "I mean, I just want you to know, as much as it's up to me, things will be different."

"I know." Flounder smiled, and it was the first time he hadn't seemed afraid. Maybe there was more to their new-found friendship than met the eye. Maybe he would miss traveling and want to leave someday. Or maybe he would stick around and help her become a better Protector than even she thought she could be.

"Okay, so here." She pointed to the tarp, considering the names. "We need to investigate them all, but with which one do we start?"

They stared and paced. Ariel sifted through the notes she and Flounder had made. There was no crystal clear way to know which of the Residents could have fiddled with the seal.

"We're stuck."

"At six suspects." It was Perla, finally! Ariel hadn't even heard the door open.

"What are we missing?" She pulled the kelp she had found in Mala's room out of her pocket and read between tiny smudges. " 'What could have saved Mother could save me, too.'

"Perla, what could have saved Mother?" Her sister remembered more of their mother, so maybe she knew.

But Perla shook her head. "I'm coming up empty. I don't know. And Father was so hush-hush about things then. I only know where she died because of the—"

"Headstone erected in the memorial." The memorial where Mother had actually died was different from the ones in the other sea territories. It was in the Fracus Sea, and it was the largest and most grand. Gems mined from sea caves were worked into the statue of Mother where her eyes would have been, and seaflora was knotted through holes in the porous rock, which made it look like hair. It was said the way the light hit just made it all the more special. Oh, how she wished she could see it herself someday. Growing up, Ariel had heard stories of seafolk who'd loved the queen. Even those who weren't fans of Father's reign.

"I don't see how I can figure out what could have saved Mother . . . without knowing more about her death," Ariel said. "And all we know is the *where*." She'd made peace with her job of bringing smiles to others instead of needling for details of Mother's death. But this message from Mala was the only clue she had. She had to follow up on it.

"Fracus Sea." Perla sighed.

Tamika's territory.

Tamika's not showing for Ariel's ceremony hadn't been a surprise, but it had disappointed her all the same. Could going to where Mother had died help her understand more about the death no one would ever talk about directly? She hoped so. Ariel knew what she had to do. Though she didn't like it.

"Get back to your room and get your FastFins, Perla."

"We're sneaking out again?"

"I can tote Flounder with me," Ariel said, ignoring her sister's obvious question.

"W-wait, I can really stay here i-if—"

"I'm not sure anyone knows more about the sea than you, Flounder. And I don't know exactly what I'm looking for out there, but I can't afford to miss an inkling of anything. I need you with me, please."

He took a breath but nodded, and she knew she was asking a lot of him. "Thank you."

"Ariel, where are we going?" Perla asked.

She drew a circle around their destination on her list of territories. "To Fisher's Kitchen—to scope out the place where Mother died."

After Perla returned with her FastFins, the group set out. Fortunately, their father was busy with the investigation, so they were able to sneak out of the castle with relative ease. Fracus Sea was the closest territory to their home, which only made it all the more odd and unsettling that Tamika never visited. But as close as it was, it was entirely different from the castle and even more different from Carinae.

Where Ariel's territory had been bright, warm, and colorful, Fracus's waters were *hot*. The fish, Ariel noticed, had great big wide gills—to breathe better in the warmer climate, she guessed. Instead of rainbow reefs and schools of shimmery fish, there were cavernous pits beneath them. Parts of the seabed looked like underground mountains, and everything was brown, orangey red, and yellow, as if the sun had drowned itself and scorched the whole place. She tried to picture her mother there all alone in her final moments, with such desolation to look upon, so far from the comfort of home.

"Did you hear the news?" said a tilapia to a gathered group of stingrays grazing under a sunlit patch of the seabed. Ariel inclined her ear. "The king is turning Fracus into a trash zone where he sends everyone he doesn't like to rot!"

The stingrays' mouths fell open in shock.

"No, I'd heard it was bad, but that's the worst," said one of the stingrays. "Every day I wish I could pack up to go to Saithe. Far away from here. But I'm restricted, so . . ."

They tsked, and Ariel bit the inside of her cheek. She wanted to stop and ask where they'd heard such lies! Ariel closed her ears and shoved down the nausea at such disturbing whispers. Perla gritted her teeth as they passed. They didn't have time to stop and talk to the fish, but what was there to say to them? Would they believe her? She wasn't sure. But it wasn't good.

The scene of the accident where her mother died was wreathed in rust-colored seaflora. The whole area looked as if it had been preserved, untouched in honor of her memory. But to Ariel it resembled a scorched nightmare. She lifted the rope sectioning off the area. Perla and Flounder swam to her side.

"It's been so long . . . years, I believe." Perla's wrists found each other like magnets, as if she was sitting with her sadness over Mother fully for the first time. Being in Fisher's Kitchen wasn't like being at the memorial back in High Sun. To swim through the space where Mother had spent her last moments shook Ariel in a way that couldn't be put into words.

Remember why you're here, she thought. What could have saved Mother? She couldn't answer that question without knowing more about Mother's death. And the only way to find that out was to search the place she died. She wasn't sure what it had to do with Mala, either, but if her sister had left her that note, it must have been important. Perhaps she'd unearth some indication of which Resident was connected to Mala's kidnapping? Grief blurred the pieces of the puzzle she tried to fit together. She could only hope following Mala's words would lead her where she needed to go.

"Maybe there is something left here from that day that could give us a clue as to what happened?" Ariel cleared her throat. "Let's find what we're looking for and get back before Father notices."

"I'll search under the debris," Perla said, stiffening her chin.

"I'll check around down below." Flounder dug his body down into the sand, unleashing a cloud of particles. "See if there's anything that's gotten buried over time underneath."

"Good idea. I'll see what I can find over this way," Ariel said, pointing at a cluster of boulders that flanked the memorial. She swam between them, not quite sure what she was looking for in the crevices. Rocks of all shapes and sizes were dotted among the plants. A few larger ones looked chipped, with sharp lines carved into their hard surfaces. She studied the divots and spotted a pile of debris on top of broken planks of wood. She sifted through it only to find a bunch of fish, unsettled by her nosiness.

"*Sorry!*" she apologized, and the fish hurried away.

Ariel continued to search through broken bits of coral and moved an entire flat of wood. By the time she had over-turned every bit of debris, her arms hurt from all the heavy lifting. Perla swam over to her, also empty-handed.

"Nothing," her sister said. "It's like Mother was never even here."

Ariel swallowed. "There must be something. We just have to find it."

Perla frowned. "I don't think there is, sis. It's been so long."

"No, there *has* to be!" Ariel said, her voice louder than she intended. She realized her nails had dug half-moons into her arm around her bracelet. She quickly released her grip and recomposed herself. Ariel plopped down on a rock. "I just meant, we can't stop. Mala's depending on us."

"Ariel." Perla's voice was kind as she sat down next to Ariel and wrapped a reassuring arm around her. "It's okay."

"But it's not, is it?" Ariel regretted the words the minute they spilled out. It was an unfair question to put to her sis-ter. A question without a real answer. And even if it had an answer, it wasn't helpful.

She closed her eyes and brought Mala to mind. What had she been thinking, coming here?

Perla squeezed her shoulder, and Ariel felt the warmth in her kind gaze. "You're too hard on yourself—"

"*Ahhh!*" Flounder's shrill cry interrupted Perla. Ariel swam up before she knew which direction she was even going. It was too dark to see fully, but she could make out Flounder a few feet away with his head buried in a stretch of overgrown seagrass.

"Flounder!" Ariel rushed over and grabbed him by the bottom half, pulling back.

"Owwwww!" he howled.

"What is it? Are you—" But the minute his head emerged, she spotted the source of the pain. A tiny creature with razor-sharp teeth and menacing eyes was clamped on his nose. It turned a single beady eye to Ariel.

"Oh, my goodness!" She jumped back.

"*Oi-do-nus!*" Flounder flapped his fins.

"What?" She pulled harder to get Flounder out of the fish's clutches.

"*OI-DO-NUS!*" Flounder shouted again, but it was all muffled under the clamp of its bite. He wriggled, trying to pull away. Ariel tugged with all her might until the fish popped off and swam away. Flounder's nose looked like a red jellyfish.

"Are you okay?" she managed.

"Poi-so-nous! Lippafish a-are poisonous!" He scrambled backward, still shouting. "Hurry, let's get out of here!"

Somewhere Perla shrieked, and out from the grass charged a rush of lippafish like the one that had been clamped on Flounder's nose. She snatched up Flounder and held him tight to her.

"Perla!" She turned to look for her sister but came face to face with an entire school of lippafish. They were surrounded.

Chapter
9

Three Days Until the Coral Moon

Asong, high like a chime playing through a string of cockle shells, rippled through the sea. Ariel looked for the source of the sound and spotted Perla, with her hand on her diaphragm, letting out the shrill melody. The lippafish froze in place, stunned by her sister's song. Her *MerSong*. Ariel had heard her hum it, but never use it against someone before.

"Are you okay?" Ariel asked Flounder.

Flounder nodded. "Lippa are poisonous, but not deadly to fish. Mermaids, though . . ."

He trailed off, and Ariel gulped. She swam over to Perla, Flounder following close behind.

"How long will this last?

But Perla couldn't respond, her mouth wide open holding the notes of her MerSong. Her chest heaved as she strained to keep the melody going, freezing the threat in place. But her strength was waning. When her Song stopped, the swarm of fish could continue their attack. Ariel wasn't sure how to help. Without her own Song, she felt a bit useless, but she had to do something.

Before Ariel could think of a plan, she spotted elongated tusks and teeth twice the size of her head charging at her. She quickly moved out of the way, pulling Flounder and Perla with her.

"I have you!" She tightened her grip on them, and the shrill sound of her sister's MerSong stopped. Perla was beside her, frozen in fear, and the lippa were slowly coming out of their comatose state.

A massive tail slithered past them, loosening a cloud of dust that obscured their vision. Words stuck in her throat. She'd led them all the way to the Fracus Sea, alone. And they were under attack by tiny fish with razor teeth and *more*. It was her fault.

"We have to get out of here!" Perla clung to her. "That *thing* is gonna devour us!"

"I—I actually think . . . it's . . . helping. Is that . . ." Flounder's words echoed the confusion radiating through Ariel. As the sand settled around them, Ariel could see that the lippa had all scattered. In their place was a creature unlike any Ariel had ever seen. Its body curved like a snake but was sharp like a swordfish. It floated in front of the lippa, bright red eyes narrowed above its tusks and gigantic teeth.

A Sea Monster.

He turned in her direction, baring his sharklike teeth, and Ariel froze. *Get out of here!* But her tail wouldn't move. He was at least three times her size.

"Please," the Sea Monster said. "Don't be afraid."

It took a moment to realize the sea creature was actually talking to them. Ariel backed away. The only Sea Monster she'd ever known was Usengu. She wasn't sure how to feel. Father's wariness of outsiders nudged her, but her heart ticked steadily. He wasn't doing anything that suggested he was going to hurt her. Still, she didn't move.

"I'm Silius. Resident in Fracus Sea," the Sea Monster continued. "You're our Protector's sisters, aren't you? The king's daughters."

Ariel's heart raced, but she blew out a breath and made herself process his words. "Y-you got rid of those lippa?"

"Indeed."

"Oh, yeah . . ." Flounder whispered to Ariel. "I've heard

about him and those giant tusks. I should've recognized him."

Ariel let go of Flounder but kept him close. Silius was one of their suspects. And he hadn't been ruled out, but at least he didn't seem to want to cause them any immediate harm.

"My apologies," Silius went on. "Security is kept tight around here. Their orders were to fend off anyone unfamiliar."

"Thank you," Perla said, still a bit shaken, lingering behind them.

"Yes, thank you very much," Ariel said. "Those lippa gave us quite the scare."

"Wait a minute, you must be the king's littlest fry." Silius kept a distance, but his voice was kind. "Haven't seen you in some time. Last time you were hiding behind your mother's fin."

Ariel tingled all over, and Silius eyed her up and down. It was weird when people could remember pieces of her life she couldn't. "You've met my mother?"

"I did. She asked me for a favor many years ago. The queen was quite lovely. I'm so sorry for your loss, Princess." He bowed his giant head. "What brings you to Fracus?"

Ariel tried to focus on his eyes when he talked and not his formidable teeth. She struggled with how to answer him. She couldn't let on that they were investigating her mother's death, especially if he had anything to do with Mala's disappearance. "We, um, well, our sister Tamika is here, and—"

"You've spoken with Tamika?" His eyes narrowed.

"No, um, but we were, uh, hoping to catch her." Ariel smiled her most convincing smile, but she couldn't meet his eyes.

"Hmm." Silius still looked skeptical. "Well, if you talk to her, please let her know I'd like an audience with her as well."

"Wait," Perla said. "You haven't seen her, either?"

"I haven't. Not in years. She's been holed up in her palace since . . . well, since this memorial was erected, if you get my drift." His gaze sank to the floor. "I don't mean to bring up something so . . . so difficult. The queen was greatly loved in Fracus. *Is* still greatly loved."

"It's all right." Ariel felt her shoulders sink a bit. "When was the last time you saw Tamika? Are you sure she's okay?"

"Oh, she's ruling, overseeing some things. We pass scrolls back and forth to communicate. She's *very* careful about who she allows to see her at close quarters and rarely hosts an audience. No one can visit. She shows her face once in a while, and she mediates trade disputes and sets security rotation schedules. But I have a bunch of worried fishfolk right now. We heard the king's rounding up some seafolk, and the Sea Monsters here fear it'll be them. I was hoping the princess could speak to their concerns, but she's not responded to my request." He threw up his fins in surrender. "Don't get me wrong, I'm not trying to tell on her by any means."

"No, no, of course not," Ariel said.

"The seafolk in Fracus love Tamika. A buddy of mine was telling me just the other day how grateful he was for the volunteers she sent to help when his home was destroyed by a rip current. She is really thoughtful. Tenderhearted." He sighed and pressed his fin to a soft spot beside his eyes. It pulsed pink. "The last time I saw her was to sort out a trade that had gone wrong between some of my brethren."

"You mean . . . other beasts like you?" Perla asked.

His chin rose, and Ariel could have sworn he flinched at her sister's words.

"Sea Monsters, I should have said," Perla amended.

"No need to apologize. The princess just used the colloquial term."

"No, she should," Ariel said, to which Perla pressed her lips closed. Just because it was the usual term didn't mean Silius liked it. And shouldn't they call him what he wanted to be called?

"We go by Oloxums, if you want to be technical. We are cousins to whale sharks and sea elephants." His lips split again, and she could see all his teeth, but from the way the corners turned up she realized he was smiling.

"I've never met an Oloxum before," Ariel said.

"Me neither," Perla muttered.

"No, you wouldn't have. Our species is rare, even for Sea Monsters. Usengu thought I'd be the perfect fit to liaise for Tamika because of how big I am and the vastness of Fracus. I have a few cousins here and there. I'm grateful for the memory ability the king gave me so I can stay close with them." His countenance rose even more then, and it warmed Ariel. He was proud of his accomplishments. As he should have been.

She cleared her throat. "Memory ability, you said?" Was that what the pink spot glowing beside his eyes was?

"Memory, that's right." Flounder nodded. "I knew it was something like that!"

Ariel had almost forgotten he was tucked under her arm. But he'd apparently warmed up to Silius a bit, too, because he wriggled himself free and swam a little closer to the Sea Monster. *Hmm.* Silius was so kind, so forthright. Could he really be a suspect in her sister's disappearance? She had to see reason. She couldn't rule out anyone just because they were likable. She'd just met him. He could . . . be putting on a good show, maybe? She couldn't take risks with their investigation. Mala's life was on the line. And possibly the throne.

But . . . if he wasn't involved, could this memory ability be useful for finding Mala?

"How does it work, exactly?" she asked.

"I can store memories inside things—shells, hollowed-out tubes of some plants," he explained. "Your father knew Oloxum are scattered and rare these days, so the ability gives me all the inherited memories from my ancestors. I can see their lives in a blink. Every single moment of each of them. And all the moments I've had over the years." Silius picked up a nearby shell, tapped his head, pulled a glowing purple bead from it, and planted in the shell. "I can also share them with others by storing them inside objects. It's quite easy. You can witness the moment I last spoke to your sister for yourself, if you'd like." He offered her the memory.

"No, that's not necessary." Ariel gazed quizzically at the shell. What a neat gift. "I believe you. That's very impressive."

"Wow," Flounder breathed. Perla swam a bit closer, her mouth ajar. An ache of sorrow hooked in Ariel's stomach. *Imagine being able to know Mother's memories.* Perla squeezed her hand and offered a smile, apparently sensing what she had been thinking.

"It is," Silius agreed. "But you know every gift has its

drawbacks. If I ever leave the boundaries of Fracus, I lose them all."

This news surprised Ariel. Was that why Father had given him such a powerful ability? To tether him there? Or had he truly done it altruistically? She wanted to believe it was the latter, not the former.

"So that means you couldn't have done it," Flounder said, and then barred his mouth shut with his fins. "Oops! Sorry."

"I'm sorry, I don't understand." Silius frowned. "Done what, exactly?"

Flounder was right: Silius could not have fiddled with the barrier or kidnapped Mala if he couldn't leave Fracus. Ariel mentally crossed him off her list of suspects. He'd been so kind, and he had literally saved their lives. He even seemed to have only love and support for her sister. Maybe she could get his insight. She wouldn't show her full hand, just in case, but testing the waters seemed . . . okay?

"Have you heard anything about danger or trouble in the kingdom? Anything about our sister Mala?" Ariel asked.

Silius's whole body straightened. Due to his massive size, the water around them shifted so violently that her heart skipped a beat.

"No . . . but . . ." His fins pulled at each other nervously.

"My position is a prickly one. My loyalty is to the king, of course, and others he has put in places of authority, such as your sister, Usengu, the like. I would never want to speak out of turn or do anything to jeopardize my position. It's held for life, you see. Only ended in death."

"Of course I understand," Ariel said. "Anything you can tell us, I'd be grateful for."

"I'll just say this." He gestured for them to come closer, and Ariel did, leaving a fidgety Flounder and Perla behind her. "The rules of our world are being tested."

"Tested?" she muttered. She looked over at Perla, who appeared just as confused as she was.

Silius nodded. "And it's unsettling a *great* many. You should talk to your father about the real history of our kingdom." He bowed his head. "I would tell you more, but we really should get moving. This area is dangerous."

"Dangerous?" Ariel asked. She had thought, other than the lippa, that they were in the clear.

"Do you see those marks on the rocks over there?" Silius said. "MerHunters."

Ariel gasped. MerHunters flooded Fracus around the Coral Moon Festival. It was known, and was why Father had designated certain safe areas where mermaids were allowed to watch the annual festivities.

"They cast these heavy nets to trap your kind," he went

on. "Then, once the net's full, they send down claws, wider than a whale's mouth, to grab the net and bring it up. Sharp and lethal things. This area is known for MerHunters. I thought you would already be aware, as the Queen was . . ." His words trailed off.

Ariel felt her body go numb. MerHunters. She'd heard of them. Creatures from the above-water world looking for mermaids to steal their scales, which they apparently sold for treasure. They were only ever rumored to have appeared in the Fracus Sea. She closed her eyes and saw slashing nets cutting through scales. That was how Mother had been killed? It wasn't an accident, like Ariel had been led to believe?

Mother was . . . hunted?

"You said that this area . . . it is known for the MerHunters?" Ariel managed.

"Oh, yeah, Fisher's Kitchen. That's where it got the name," Silius said.

"Why was Mother swimming here of all places?" Ariel asked, more to herself than anyone. The keen ache she'd felt earlier twisted within her. She was about to ask Silius another question when—

"ARIEL AND PERLA, GET OVER HERE THIS MINUTE!"

Who in the—

Ariel looked in the direction of the shouting just as Indira opened her lungs and blew. Her MerSong blared against

Silius's face, and his complexion flared red as the water temperature grew to a boil.

"Stop!" Ariel shouted so loud her brain rattled. Her sister had shown up with Caspia in tow and was blaring her melody at poor Silius. "He's helping us!"

Ariel shoved Indira out of the way, and Silius returned his deep grayish-blue. He blinked, stumbling back.

"Are you okay?" Ariel asked.

"I'm fine, Princess. I'll get going. I don't want any trouble." Silius swam off before she could pull him back or even try to introduce him. Ariel faced her sisters.

"You two!" Ariel scolded. "What are you—"

"Us?" Indira pulled Ariel by the wrist, so tight it hurt. "You're upset with us? We just saved your scales!"

"You almost *hurt* someone helping us," Ariel spat.

"That scary thing?" asked Indira.

"Yes, ugh!" Ariel rolled her eyes. "How'd you even know where we were?"

"It was obvious," Indira said. "Your little investigation notes are scribbled all over your room."

Ariel bit her lip. She hadn't thought of clearing her room before they left. "Don't go in my room when I'm not there."

"We were coming to check in on you," Indira said, folding her arms. "Father feels like he's zeroing in on things."

"And, uh, your privacy is the least of your concerns," Caspia said. "We should tell Father you've snuck out!"

"You haven't already?" That surprised Ariel.

"No, we haven't, because we don't want him jumping down our throats, but you keep this up and we will," Indira said.

Ariel sighed. At least she wasn't in trouble yet. She looked around for Flounder, who had sped away when Indira and Caspia arrived. She spotted him trying to hide behind a piece of coral and gestured for him to come over. He swam to her tentatively, nervously eyeing Caspia's and Indira's scowling faces.

"Sorry for putting you in the middle of a family spat," Ariel told him.

Flounder rubbed his nose. "I-I'm fine. Just glad th-that's over."

"You guys are seriously the worst." Perla pushed past Indira and Caspia, close enough to hit both their shoulders. "I was with her. We were . . ."

Ariel cut a sharp glance at Perla to keep quiet. Indira and Caspia couldn't be trusted. Ariel knew that now beyond a doubt.

"Pretty much okay," Perla finished.

Indira put her hands on her hips. "Not from what we saw."

Ariel rolled her eyes. "Well, that Sea Monster you scared away was Silius, the Resident here, and he knows things. He gave us a warning that the rules of our world are being tested."

Was that how he worded it?

Caspia didn't look amused. "You can't be serious."

"She's totally serious. Look at her." Indira sighed, exasperated. "Can we get going? Maybe if we get back now we can actually get some sleep tonight."

"Your sleep is the least of my concerns." Ariel fumed, struggling to keep her frustration at bay. "*I'm* worried about Mala!"

"Mala isn't the model sister you think," Indira said. "She probably got herself into this mess." She huffed, and Caspia nodded. "Father will sort it out."

Ariel wasn't sure what that meant. But Indira and Caspia's feud with Mala was never-ending. That was a dead end. "And what about Karina? Did you guys notice she left in a rush? She seemed nervous about something. Doesn't that concern you? We should reach out to her. Silius—"

"Karina's late to everything and leaves early," Caspia said. "I'm not at all surprised."

It was like Ariel was talking to herself. Flounder's eyes darted between them.

"There's no use, Ari." Perla took Ariel by the elbow. It really was like talking to Father.

"M-maybe they're right and we should get back, you know . . . since it's so, u-uh, late?" Flounder's nose was still a red bulb.

Ariel felt bad. "You're right. We should get back and get that nose looked at. Some aloegae should help, I think." She huffed a sigh, accepting defeat. She wasn't going to get anywhere with her sisters that night.

Chapter
10

Three Days Until the Coral Moon

The king's castle was quiet when Ariel and her sisters snuck back in and swam to their individual rooms. She couldn't shake Silius's words from her memory. What did he mean, the rules of their world were being tested? What rules exactly? Relating to Sea Monsters? To Protectors? Something else?

"Princess Ariel, is that you?" one of the king's guards called, and Ariel swam faster, realizing her room was likely still a mess. The last thing she wanted was a guard to see any of the things she'd collected to help with the investigation and take them away from her.

They hurried to keep up with her, but their shell armor made their movements clunkier. She threw her door open and shoved her suspect list and all the mess she'd made into a woven seaweed basket. She hid it under her bed just as the guards entered. They looked at her, and she met their stares with hard determination.

"Yes, well? Trying to get some sleep, if you don't mind." She spotted the net she'd gathered from the memorial in Carinae across the room, strewn across her bed. *Oh, carp!* She thought she'd grabbed everything. If they didn't look around, they wouldn't see it.

"The king said everyone should be in bed. We are under orders to keep everyone in their rooms until further notice. No roaming the castle, Princess." The swordfish's eyes narrowed, combing her in suspicion. "And no visitors, either." He scanned, and she knew he was looking for Flounder.

"He's in his own room. If there's not anything else, please go." She bit back the guilt twisting inside her. She felt bad for raising her voice at the guards. That was a first, but she was getting tired of people not listening. The guards retreated, and she collapsed in relief on her bed. Thank goodness. She wouldn't be held off from figuring out what Silius was referring to. Somehow it led to Mala, she just knew it.

She checked the window in her room. The sun would be up soon, which meant they had only two more days to find

Mala. Would Father really give up his throne in exchange for her if they failed to find her first? Was that how the kidnapper intended this to go? The note hadn't been very clear. Could they even trust they would honor the exchange if it came to that? Ariel spiraled. She couldn't imagine Father entertaining either of these options—not finding Mala or giving up his throne. Her eyes were heavy and she let them bat a beat longer than she intended. She had no time for sleep, not when her sister was in danger.

Should I try to get back in touch with Silius? She wanted to sift through the things they'd found once more. But she couldn't risk pulling out all her doodads and her father or his guards finding her. So many things to do, and yet it felt like the king's eyes were over her shoulder. She chewed her lip so hard it hurt. The next thing she felt was restless sleep.

Tap tap tap.

Ariel swam up at the sound. She yawned the sleep from her eyes. How long had she been out?

Tap tap tap.

"Who's there?" she asked. Ariel looked around but saw no one. Then she realized the noise was coming from her window. Ripples of sunlight streamed into her room, and a plate of food sat on her whalebone desk.

Tap tap tap.

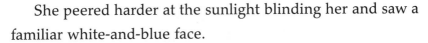

She peered harder at the sunlight blinding her and saw a familiar white-and-blue face.

"Flounder!"

She shoved the glass open.

"Hey!" he said. He swam inside.

"Hey! Why are you entering through the window?"

"I tried coming to visit you earlier, but the guards wouldn't let me. There are more of them today than there were yesterday," Flounder said. "But I wanted to see you, so I asked Scuttle, my bird friend, to distract the guards outside the castle. She dove down and plucked something from one of them, and they followed her."

Ariel's heart sank. Either her father knew they had snuck out last night, or he was becoming even more cautious with Mala missing. How was she supposed to help if she was stuck inside?

"Well, if the guards are still near the surface, we better get moving before they come back," Ariel said. "There is no time to waste."

Flounder frowned. "O-oh, Ariel. I—I don't want any more trouble. I—I was just hoping to come talk to you is all. I thought I'd sneak back into my room by lunch." He grabbed his tummy.

"I just want find a place for all these things before

someone else sees them," Ariel said. She held up her suspect board. "Somewhere where Father can't find it." *Or my nosy sisters.*

"I—I, uh, may sit this one out."

"Oh, come on, please." She gathered the net, the broken bits of rock, the tangled seaweed, and the rest of the "junk" she'd gathered and hidden in her room over the years. She barred the door shut and wedged some clutter behind it. They'd think she was sleeping in since she had been up so late. "It'll be quick."

Flounder looked around, as if looking for a reason for them to stay. When he couldn't find one, he sighed. "All right, I guess."

She squeezed his fin in appreciation. "We'll be back before Father knows a thing, promise!"

After checking to make sure there were no guards around, Ariel and Flounder swam around until they finally came across a hollowed-out cave beneath a clatter of shipwrecked wood. Its opening tunnel was full of barbs and barnacles, and working their way through them was trickier than it looked. But being hard to access was a good thing. Inside, the cave was lined with naturally made shelves as far as her eyes could see. Up top, there was an opening where sunlight winked at her.

"Are you sure you want to leave your stuff out here?" Flounder asked, dusting the shelves cut into the rock with his fins.

It was a solid three whalebones from her castle. "Better chance Father won't stumble upon it, don't you think?"

"Couldn't you just maybe tell him everything you know? That seems a bit safer, to me."

"Flounder, I tried talking to Father, but you saw how stubborn he is. He doesn't listen." She held up a glassy orb she'd found rolling around the ocean floor on their journey to the grotto. What was it? Did it do something? She pressed on it, but it was hard and didn't give. She held it to her eye, but couldn't see anything beneath its foggy surface. Still, she set it on a shelf.

"Hello?" A voice rippled through the grotto, echoing against the walls. Ariel ducked behind a rock. Flounder's eyes bulged as he joined her.

"We were followed," Ariel whispered. Her heart leapt in her chest as she looked for something sharp she could use to defend them if need be.

"Ariel?" Perla moved from beneath the shadow, pulling herself out of the narrow tunneled entryway.

"Perla! What are you doing out of the castle?"

"I saw you duck out of your room from my window and followed," Perla said. "But goodness, girl, you swim fast. What is this place, anyway?" Her neck swiveled, and she picked up a shiny silver thing Ariel had found stuck in an anemone once.

"Somewhere we can meet without Father discovering what we're up to," Ariel said. "Have you heard any updates?"

Perla shook her head. "Julia came by to bring me some food this morning. She seemed really shaken up with every- thing going on. She told me Father and some of his guards are out searching and questioning local Sea Monsters with High Sun connections, but that they haven't found anything connected to Mala yet."

Ariel sighed. He wasn't even on the right track. She had hoped that maybe her father had found some clues during his search.

"What about Karina?" Ariel asked. "Has she sent any news? She left in such a hurry yesterday. Do you think she knows something?"

Perla paused, considering the suspect board. "You know, it didn't seem relevant before, but maybe . . . No, it's prob- ably nothing."

"Tell us!" Ariel and Flounder said at the same time.

"Well . . ." Perla squinted as if the words were tangled in

her memory. "So when Karina and I were arguing the other day—you know, when we showed up for the ceremony?"

Ariel nodded.

"Karina had mentioned a boat crashed in Bone Reef recently, which is this shallower area on the northernmost tip of Saithe Sea, her territory. She said it was loaded up with all kinds of nets and hooks, like the kind Silius was describing that cut those rocks."

"Bone Reef?" Flounder's eyes had grown to twice their size. "They call it the Ice Graveyard. Rumors are the waters are so cold there in some parts just touching it can freeze you to death." He shuddered.

Perla nodded. "Karina wanted to tell Father about the crash when we were waiting for your Protector Ceremony to start. She thought the boat might be connected to MerHunters, but I didn't want her to mention anything that could ruin your ceremony."

Ariel frowned.

"But, thinking about it more, if Karina was right and it was indeed a MerHunter boat," Perla said, "how did they know to look for merfolk in Saithe in the first place? It's not a spot we've seen MerHunters venture to before. Father even lets merfolk freely watch Coral Moon festivities from those waters."

Perla was right. MerHunters only ever frequented two

other places in the ocean, neither of which was near Saithe.

Ariel fiddled with a pokey gizmo on her shelf, the pieces of the puzzle cinching together in her brain. "MerHunters *killed* Mother, and another MerHunter boat might have been in Bone Reef. Silius made it sound like something bigger was going on. Is this what he meant by the rules of the world being tested—MerHunters searching new seas? Could Mala's kidnapping have something to do with this?" She tapped her lip. "Could MerHunters have dove underwater and taken Mala with their own bare hands instead of using their net and claw thingy?" Ariel felt like she was trying to peer through muddied water.

Perla frowned. "But if Mala knew she was being taken by MerHunters, why wouldn't she just say that on her note? Why be so cryptic?"

"Right," Flounder said. "And a MerHunter couldn't break the king's barrier. Only a Resident could have taken Mala."

"Well, if that boat wreck in Saithe was MerHunters, their MerHunter friends will definitely go looking for their lost buddies," Ariel said. "We have to at least check on things in Saithe and warn Karina. And while we're there, see if there's any evidence in Bone Reef tying this to Mala's disappearance somehow."

"Ariel, we can't go to Bone Reef! Father's guards will be back and know we are missing," Perla argued.

"Saithe is extremely treacherous." Flounder shook his head emphatically. "The arctic temperatures there alone make it really unsafe for some seafolk. I—I can't . . ."

Indira's Song Mother taught her warms everything in the sur-rounding area. If she'd come with us . . . She'd never. We're on our own. But Karina won't be.

Ariel shouldered her seaweed bag, her mind made up. Their trip to Fracus had been enlightening. She *had* to see what answers Bone Reef held, too. "Flounder, you can go back to the castle and cover for us." She turned to Perla. "I hope you don't mind the cold."

Chapter 11

Two Days Until the Coral Moon

Bone Reef was unlike anything Ariel had seen. Karina was always pale, and now Ariel understood why. The ocean was much darker than it was where she grew up. Despite its still being the afternoon, very little sunlight shone through from the surface. She pushed through the water, gritting her teeth, against a current that wrapped around her like a hug of ice.

Still, she couldn't deny that Saithe was a wonder all its own. Icy flora sparkled in the dimness like an underwater night sky. She hugged herself, rubbing the tiny bumps up her arm. She was cold—a cold that cut through her skin, deep into her bones. She tried to get a peek above the water, but chunks of ice sat on the surface, keeping them buried underneath. *Am I going the right way? I hope so.*

The seabed was a nest of algae and reefs, glowing deep blue and purple. She realized she was squinting as they passed sea creatures, many she'd never seen. They all had really large eyes, because of the dark waters, she assumed. They said nothing to her or Perla as they swam past. And despite feeling like she should be friendly, she was too frazzled to say anything to them.

"It should be somewhere around here, I think," Ariel said. She tried to remember all the maps of the different seas she had studied while preparing to become a Protector. As she looked around for any familiar landmarks, she noticed a stream of bubbles shooting up like an underwater hot spring. A fish loitered nearby, rubbing its fins together. It reminded her of the baths they had at the castle. Father had them designed just for the family to keep warm on particularly cool nights. It appeared Karina had taken that idea and made something similar for the creatures in her territory. Ariel pointed it out, and Perla's eyes snapped that way. "Clever, huh?"

But Perla wasn't quick to give Karina compliments and kept silent. They swam a little farther before spotting a sign for Bone Reef. It was just up ahead, but between them and it was a forest of icy kelp.

Perla's teeth chattered in the cold, and Ariel swam closer to her, keeping them tight together to share body heat. White glinted at her from the seabed. She didn't have to look at it directly to know bones covered the graveyard's floor. She winced, imagining what the bones were from. They were piled in mountains, frosted on their edges and in all different sizes and shapes. Maybe this had been a mistake. The water shifted and the world darkened. The little sunlight Saithe did have wasn't out for many hours. They'd have to hurry.

"I can't believe Karina lives in this a-a-all the time," Perla said as they swam through the towers of kelp. The deeper they went, the more the shards of light from overhead disappeared, ray by ray. The swaying kelp thickened into a nest she couldn't see her way through. The world was closing in around her, and the spaces between her breaths shrank with it.

Ariel held tighter to Perla's arm. The kelp moved more violently, thrashing the water from side to side. Ariel pinched herself to calm her growing panic. Had she led her sister into danger? *Again . . . ! No, no . . . I'm just cold. Focus,* she told herself, trying to take a look around.

A glimpse of something caught her eye. She let go of Perla's arm and lurched toward it, shoving her way between the suffocating icicles. On the seafloor under a pile of bones was a net, nearly buried under rock, like the one they'd found in Fracus. Perla appeared closed behind her. Her lips were as blue as her hair, but she nodded, noticing the same thing Ariel had. *MerHunters have definitely been here.* Ariel grabbed the net and tucked it under her arm. She'd inspect it once they were in better light.

"Let's get closer to the surface. It's getting too dark down here."

Perla nodded, and Ariel led the way back up from the seabed through the nest of icicles. But the seaweed that had just been rocking in a slow hum back and forth shifted. Its icy strands wrapped around one another, tying themselves together. Ariel tried to shove through, but the icicles knotted themselves, making it impossible to get through or around them. Her head swiveled, the thump in her veins rising despite the chill in her bones. There had to be another way up from the seabed without going through the icy under-water forest.

"Watch out!" Perla shoved Ariel out of the way as a writh-ing bit of kelp curled around her wrist. Ariel tugged at the seaweed and bit back the chilly burn scorching her fingers. Cold slithered around her skin, and she gasped, contorting in the curling, icy grip. Next to her, she could just make out snow-flaked leaves gripping Perla by her torso.

"Help!" Perla called as the kelp pulled her further down. "Ariel, help!"

"Perla!" The more Ariel moved, the tighter the icy plant wove around her. She couldn't move. The plant had her in its clutches from the waist down, but she held fiercely to the net. She opened her mouth but felt a slick cold graze her throat as the icy leaf worked its way up her body, curling around her neck. She held still, fear coursing through her, and to her surprise, the plants stopped.

"Try not moving!" Ariel could barely make out her sister, who was almost fully covered by the tangle of icy weeds. Perla stopped struggling against it, and the kelp halted its assault.

"Okay, now . . . if we move really slowly, maybe we can work our way out of it." Ariel wiggled ever so slightly, and the icicle tightened on her torso. The weeds stirred beneath them.

"It hurts!"

"Shhh!" Okay, they couldn't move. There was no way out. Ariel suddenly realized why there were so many bones on the ocean floor. "Just be still. Let me think."

A tail swished in front of her before she could finish. The world spun, and several things happened at once. Ariel felt the grip on her chest tighten. Something flashed white. And then Ariel felt the plant's leaves let her go. She was being carried by someone, pulled against the water, so fast she could hardly move. Water rushed past them; whoever was pulling her was doing so at lightning speed. The farther away she was carried, the warmer she felt. She blinked, and she could feel her face again, move her arms. Heat crept into her fingers, and she wiggled them.

She blinked again, and there was Perla. She too was clutched around the wrist by a familiar mermaid with light purple hair.

"Karina?" Ariel managed.

Her sister smiled.

It was her! Ariel would have thought she'd imagined it if it hadn't been for the coarse net still tangled around her hands. But there she was, a cascade of lilac hair down her back. "But how did you kno—"

"*Shhh.* Save your strength until we're inside."

Karina held on to their hands as she swam them away from Bone Reef and to the Saithe palace. The entrance to the palace was flanked with pillars sculpted with designs like hand-carved snowflakes. Glass panes slid open upon their approach. Once they were inside, Karina released them, and it took a second for the world to stop spinning.

"Are you okay?" Karina held Perla by the shoulders as she

shivered. Then she tapped a school of tuna, who glowed and started moving around the room, heating the water around them.

"I think so," Perla said. Her pale lips moved slowly.

"The chill will wear off." Karina gave her a reassuring smile. "I'll be right back."

Her sister left them in the vestibule. Ariel couldn't remember the last time she had seen Karina and Perla talking to each other without bickering. And actually *helping* each other? That might have been a first. Ariel pulled the MerHunter's net onto her lap and tugged at its strands carefully. There were all sorts of trash stuck in its fibers. She fiddled with a large knot, undoing it and letting the trash fall to the floor. Then she spotted a scrap of paper. Sketched on the torn paper were various underwater locations.

A map?

She turned the scrap, looking at it from different angles. It did seem to be a map of some sort, like the ones she had studied back in her father's castle. Or a piece of one, rather. Ariel chewed off her nail. The map showed Humpback Hollow in Chaine Sea and Starry Pass in Brinedive Sea, places mermaids frequented because they were considered safe. Were MerHunters using the map to target mermaids? She couldn't see any reason someone would be in those treacherous waters unless they had a specific purpose. She stared at it a bit longer, Perla's shivering slowing down next to her. She looked up, surprised her other sister had yet to return.

"Karina, is everything okay?" Ariel called. She swam out of the room and back to the hall. She heard a noise coming from behind the double doors nearby. Ariel pushed through them and gasped.

It was the castle foyer, with tunnels that looked like they led to various levels of Saithe palace, but it was a wreck. It appeared to have been completely ransacked. Light orbs lay shattered all over the floor. Broken tables; overturned furniture; ripped tarps, half hanging from the windows. Ariel stared in shock.

"I asked you to wait in the entry," Karina called. She emerged from one of the tunnels, her cheeks pink with embarrassment.

"Karina, what happened?" It was Perla, who had followed Ariel.

"Nothing. It's fine." Karina glared at them, kicking back some debris on the floor with the bottom of her tail. "I just need to clean up around here."

"What is going on?" Ariel moved closer to her sister, who was trembling.

"Please," Perla said. "Are you hurt? Did someone—"

"No!" Karina snapped. She paused, looking down at the

floor before letting out a sigh. "When I returned home from Carinae, it was like this. Some Sea Monster must have broken in. I have no idea who, or why, honestly. I do my best to oversee things here, meeting their needs, and—"

"Why didn't you say something?" Ariel was aghast.

"And have Father take the responsibility away from me?" Karina scoffed. "Or have Perla, Indira, and Caspia gloat at how bad I am at this whole Protector thing?"

"There's nothing you could have done to prevent this, Karina," Perla said.

"Perla's right," Ariel said, then blinked in disbelief. Was Perla actually not taking digs at Karina?! "You weren't here. You can't be held responsible for this."

Karina squeezed Ariel's arm affectionately, and she warmed all over, taking the moment in. It was really happening. Despite the chaos swimming around them and Mala's being missing, two of her sisters had buried the harpoon. Karina's lip trembled as she held in a dam of emotions.

"It's okay." Perla pulled her into a hug, and Karina broke, wailing louder, her wrists rubbing together in sadness.

"You can't tell Father," Karina said.

"We would never," Ariel said, wrapping around them. She'd never seen Karina worked up that way. And she'd certainly never seen Perla so serious. "This will be our secret. But we have to find out who is behind it."

"That's the thing," Karina said. "The only people who have access to the palace are my serving staff and my Resident."

"Have you asked them if they saw anything?"

"Most of my staff is away preparing for the Coral Moon. I've been too scared to even go outside. The only reason I did today is because I heard some fish whispering about strangers swimming around near Bone Reef. About that!" She pulled herself out of their hug and bore into Ariel. "*What* were you thinking, Lula? Bone Reef *earned* its name."

"I'm sorry," Ariel said. "I'm just determined to figure out what happened to Mala. Father's being shortsighted and won't include us. So we wanted—"

"*You* wanted," Perla corrected. "I just came along to make sure you didn't get yourself killed. Which, I mean . . ."

"Fine. *I* wanted to go to the spot Mother died because of that note Mala left us on the kelp. And then I heard about the crash here and got curious if the two were connected." Ariel shifted with embarrassment, realizing how foolish she'd been to venture into such dangerous waters a second time. "I guess somewhere deep down I'd hoped Mala would be there or something. That we'd find her."

It sounded so stupid, aloud. So naive. Perhaps she wasn't cut out for leading a territory after all. Perhaps she did need Sebastian as a babysitter.

"The only thing you'll find in Bone Reef are bones," Karina

chastised. "I don't know where Mala is, but if she were in my territory, I'd be aware."

"I mean this in the gentlest way," Perla began. "But it seems like there's stuff happening in Saithe that you actually *don't* know about, sis. Someone clearly wishes you ill. I mean, look around."

Perla's words reminded Ariel of what Silius had said. She looked up at her sister. "Karina, can you tell us why you left so abruptly? In High Sun?"

"After hearing about Mala being taken, you mean?" Her tone deadened and she turned her back to them. Ariel and Perla shared a glance.

"I saw Mala that morning. She said something. Before she—" She shook her head, her voice cracking. "Now, every time I close my eyes I see her. Like a ghost that won't leave me alone."

Ariel set a hand on Karina's shoulder. "You can tell us. You don't have to carry whatever it is alone."

Karina gazed between them with uncertainty.

"Go on," Perla said. "It's okay."

"I just feel so bad in hindsight. I . . . I didn't really listen when she was talking, you know? I was more annoyed that she was in my room trying to borrow my hair pearl." Karina blew out a breath. "It all seems so trivial in retrospect. But she mentioned she was going to let someone inside the seal.

It was a surprise she was planning for your ceremony. She wouldn't say more."

Ariel remembered Mala's mischievous grin the last time Ariel had seen her. How was Mala planning to open the seal? Only a Resident or her father could mess with the barrier. Had Mala asked a Resident to help her? Could that be the same Resident who took her?

"I just didn't think about it," Karina went on. "But when Mala came up missing . . . it scared me. I don't know. Maybe I felt guilty, too. I wanted to get back home. Somewhere that felt safe."

Home. There was that word again. At some point, home had been her father's palace. But their homes away from home had encroached on that idea, taking it over like a cluster of barnacles. Home was unrecognizable from the place they'd known when Mother's singing filled the halls. But in Saithe, at her palace, Karina was away from the memories of Mother, the rooms that used to hold her voice, the staff who knew her smile. Here, she didn't need to face her grief.

"Then I got here and saw this, and that just—"

"Scared you even more," Perla finished for her.

Karina nodded. "I'm so ashamed."

"Don't be," Ariel said. "Mother's death left its marks on all of you guys, in different ways."

"This has nothing to do with Mother," Karina insisted.

It had everything to do with Mother, Ariel would have bet. So much had to do with Mother, she realized. But she wasn't going to argue with her sister. She'd have to help them see, carefully, gently.

"Speaking of Mother, we think she was . . ." The words stuck in her throat. "Actually harmed by MerHunters." She reached for the torn map she had found in the net, but Karina's gaze fell. Her sister bit her lip, and Ariel frowned.

"You knew?" Ariel asked.

Karina nodded slowly. "I knew. Mala and I figured it out once we learned Mother died in Fracus where the MerHunters are known to sail, but I'm not sure if the others did. Indira and Caspia . . . well, we don't talk, so. What about you, Perla?"

Perla shook her head, her mouth ajar in shock.

What else had her older sisters kept from her? Ariel sighed. They didn't have time to question Karina about that. They had to put all their energy into finding Mala. "I found this piece of a map in a MerHunter net. Do you think it could have something to do with the Resident who took Mala?"

"Wait, a Resident took Mala?" Karina asked.

"We're pretty sure," Perla said, and updated her on the broken seal they'd found and Silius's warning.

"But that still doesn't explain the MerHunters or this map I found." Ariel frowned. She looked down at the scrap in her hands. Then she froze. Blood pushed through her. Her pulse sped up. No one from the surface could have known the places listen on the map. Only seafolk.

Unless . . .

Oh, gosh.

"Is it possible that the Resident who took Mala is also responsible for letting the MerHunters know where merfolk live?" Ariel asked.

Their eyes darted around the room, hesitant to pin down one theory, chase it with all they had, and end up wrong. *That would mean MerHunters are working with someone from the sea.* But Ariel had never heard of a sea creature being able to speak with surface beings. How would they even communicate? Was that even possible?

"But the ransom note made it sound like the kidnapper was among those up in arms about Father's reign," Perla said, worry written into her expression. "Why would MerHunters hate Father or want him to give up the throne?"

"I don't know." Ariel's shoulders sagged, and she steadied herself on a wall. Perla had a good point. Ariel felt like she was holding pieces of a puzzle that seemed to shift depending on the angle she looked at them. And she didn't feel great about any of it. Seafolk in Father's kingdom working with MerHunters? Was that really what was happening? She felt sick.

What do I know? What do I know for sure?

"We can help you clean up a bit," Perla offered, and Ariel nodded, going along with it. She needed to think. She swished a pile of clutter with her tail until it was in a short stack and she could see the floor again. *Silius was right.* The rules of their world were being tested. Nerves still twisted in Ariel's stomach. But what was causing it? She would find out.

Chapter 12

Two Days Until the Coral Moon

Ariel and Perla helped Karina fix up the messy foyer for the better part of the evening, and Ariel stewed on the map and what it could mean.

"Help me with this end, would you?" Ariel lifted the end of a stubborn piece of furniture. She looked for Perla but didn't see her. "Perla?" Still no sign of her. But Ariel did spot two beady eyes peeking at her from behind a fallen tarp. "What the—" She swam over and ripped the tarp away, which revealed a passage big enough for a ship to pass through. And hovering there in the center of it was a creature the size of a small whale.

His sloped back had two dorsal fins, and gills lined his belly. Long whiskers for helping sense the direction in the dark Saithe waters spread in every direction from his nose, and a giant blowhole was in the center of his head. Was he a Sea Monster? The sheer size of him twisted Ariel's insides, but she grabbed the sharpest thing she could find. Thanks to the broken furniture, there was no shortage of such.

"Who are you?" she demanded. "How did you get in here?"

"Tolum! You're okay!" Karina swam past Ariel toward the whale and threw her arms around his nose. Ariel bit her lip. Had she made a mistake again? Perla swam back in the room and yelped at the sight of Tolum.

"Tolum is Resident here," Karina said.

"Oh, my goodness. My apologies!" Ariel wanted to shrink on the spot. She quickly dropped her weapon, a blush spreading across her cheeks.

His head rose in pride before turning to Karina. "Yes, I'm okay, Princess. Sorry I haven't been by on my usual rounds. The sea has been a whirlwind of discontent with all the rumors about the king. Trying to keep the peace."

Perla's brow cinched in confusion at Ariel. *Rumors? How far-reaching are these whispers about Father? Have they reached Saithe? Is it spreading?*

"What's happened here? Are *you* okay?" Tolum's gaze

creased with concern as he gazed around at the foyer. Karina filled him in on the break-in, and Ariel watched as the Sea Monster doted on her sister, offering condolences and having her recount everything that had happened. Ariel hadn't expected him and Karina to have such amicable dealings. After all, he was a suspect. Was Perla like that with her Resident? Was that typical? Father had painted them so . . . differently.

How had Father described the Mer–Monster Treaty? *A necessary precaution to keep the most vile far away,* or something like that. Nothing about Tolum was vile, and that was obvious. Silius either! Father would have said it was because they were Residents. Among the few "good ones," like Usengu. Ariel wasn't sure she bought it.

"Absolutely outrageous!" Tolum shouted once Karina was done with her story. He swam in a circle, taking note of all the damage. "We will get to the bottom of this, Princess."

"Any idea who could be behind it?" Ariel asked.

"I don't have any leads off the top of my head. It could be anyone, but I'll be looking into it straightaway," Tolum said.

"Oh, of course! Please be thorough," Ariel said.

"Tensions are high between Sea Monsters and merfolk, specifically around here."

Karina nodded. "More whispers about Father every time

I look up. Usengu's been here every week trying to support Tolum and talk them down."

"Ambassador Usengu is truly a master of words." Tolum smiled. "That serpent could calm a monsoon with the right string of words. But the tensions are leading to all kinds of acting out. I've been staying with the Sea Monsters in their territory for the past few days, trying to get a handle on things." He sighed. "Though . . . it's difficult, because they are not wrong."

"Whatever do you mean?" Ariel perked up.

"It does appear Sea Monsters requests of the King, sent by way of Usengu, haven't been answered in a timely manner. Many have not been answered at all. And I fear the lack of response is being stoked into fear that the rumors about the king are in fact true."

Oh, this is complex indeed.

Karina's brows creased. Had she not heard the rumors? Ariel was relieved at least Tolum seemed to have a good pulse on the situation. She mentally crossed him off her suspect list. Tolum couldn't lie. If he had been dealing with Sea Monsters in Saithe, he couldn't have been the who had taken Mala, and his care for Karina seemed too genuine to be an act.

"To be clear, I won't jump to conclusions on who to blame for this break-in. It could be anyone, Sea Monster, merfolk, seafolk passing through. With all of these rumors floating around . . ." Tolum continued. The sisters looked at him curiously.

"What rumors exactly?" asked Karina

"Well, I've just got wind of this, so I hadn't had a chance to mention it to you, but I hear it's not just Sea Monsters upsetting the balance of things . . ."

There is that sentiment again, Ariel thought, remembering their time in Fracus. *Like Silius said.*

Tolum hesitated, and Ariel felt her heart skip a beat. "But a mermaid *and* a Sea Monster working together to do so."

Tolum's words and her mismatched clues sat on Ariel, stuck to her like a starfish for the rest of the day. She kept rolling his words around in her head, trying to make sense of them as they picked up the last bits of Karina's foyer. Somehow this all tied back to Mala. She just knew it.

When they finally finished cleaning, she tossed a sculpted shell chairback that'd been broken in half onto the mountain of trash outside Karina's palace.

"I'll put in the heavy trash request," Perla said before disappearing back inside.

"Do you both have to go so soon?" Karina's eyelids were

no longer swollen, and she'd finally stopped rubbing her wrists together. They'd even managed to wiggle a few laughs out of her as they all did their best impressions of Father trying to tell off Tolum, one of few in the ocean who could actually make the king seem small in comparison.

"We should be getting back before Father notices we've gone." Ariel hoped Flounder had been able to cover for her. "Come with us. It's probably safer. Father would love a visit. It might even perk everyone up."

Karina made a face.

"Hey, if you and Perla can get along, stranger things can happen."

They laughed.

"I should stay here and see what Tolum turns up," Karina said. "But, Ariel, this is really serious. I appreciate everything you've done to support me."

"And actually," Perla said, joining them, "I've been thinking I should probably get back to Piton and check on things. These uprisings seem to be getting worse. With everything happening here with you, Karina, it's making me think I need to get back. Soon."

"I just feel in my gut that we're zeroing in on this," Ariel said. "I need to get back to the grotto and look at everything we know laid out."

Karina's hand closed around her wrist, soft and gentle. "Sweet Lula, please put this investigation to bed."

"But we're so close."

"Someone's already got Mala. And if you're right and this is somehow connected to MerHunters, I wouldn't be able to forgive myself if something happened to either of you," Karina said. "Get home, lie low, and tell Father everything you know. Show him the map. He will take this seriously, I'm sure of it. Even if the tip came from a Resident. He knows Tolum cannot lie."

Ariel looked down, feeling a bit of guilt for the first time since starting her search. She knew her sisters cared for her and did not want her to get into trouble, but couldn't they see that it was worth the risk if she could save Mala?

"I'll think about what you said on my swim back and seriously consider talking to Father," Ariel promised. After the way her father had spoken to her the last time she'd tried to tell him about her findings, she wasn't eager to go to him with the new information, but it was worth considering if it would make Karina feel better.

"He'll listen," Karina said. "I'm telling you. He likes Tolum."

"Okay, we should get moving." Ariel hugged her sister tight. "By the way, what do *you* make of the mermaid thing Tolum said? It's concerning, isn't it?"

"I don't know, but Tolum is my right hand here. He's got a sharp sense for sniffing out trouble, and he's not a gossip." At Perla's and Ariel's troubled expressions, Karina continued, "Mala is going to come through this okay, you guys. Somehow."

"I hope so," Perla said. "And I swear I'll never ignore her annoying rambling again. And I'll braid her hair no matter how much she pesters me."

They laughed and hugged. Ariel piled on top of it, too. The hug was suffocatingly tight, her sisters' faces pressed against her own. But at that moment, there was nowhere else in the world Ariel would rather have been. *Speaking of sisters we're missing.*

"We should check on Tamika," Ariel said.

"She's a lost cause, I think," Karina said.

"So were you and Perla until today."

"But Tamika's been a stranger since Mother died," Perla said, breaking the hug to slip into her FastFins. "I don't even know who she is anymore. Some of the rumors I hear—like that sea urchins have taken over her castle . . . I wonder if there's truth to them."

Ariel hoped there wasn't. She hoped that Tamika was somehow okay, and everyone was wrong about her. Ariel secured her own FastFins, and they bid Karina goodbye.

In mere moments, Saithe was in squinting distance behind them. But Karina's and Perla's words were a buoy in Ariel's thoughts, determined to float to the forefront. Tamika might have been detached, but it didn't change who she was: Mother's daughter and *their* sister. Could she be hurting, too? Was that why she stayed away? Ariel bit her lip. *Mala. I have to find Mala.* Perhaps she would have to tackle bringing their family back together one disaster at a time.

Perla accompanied Ariel all the way to their father's palace before heading back to Piton. The castle was silent when Ariel arrived. Fortunately, it seemed the guards from earlier were off with more important tasks, so it was relatively easy to sneak back in. She swam toward her room to make sure Flounder was doing okay. She knocked on her own door.

"I'm really not feeling well," someone rasped in a high voice that Ariel realized must have been Flounder's impression of her. She laughed.

"Flounder, it's me," she said, and the door swung open. "So I'm assuming that everything went okay?"

"Oh, my goodness, I'm so glad you're back. You have any idea how insistent that housekeeper of yours is?" Flounder said, his voice back to normal. "When I told her I—well, you—didn't feel well, she had half the kitchens at the door wanting to feed me bone broth and check my scales."

Ariel laughed. Julia had been a stand-in mother for so long. "Yes, well, she takes good care of me. What did you tell her?"

"That I was too tired and not ready for company. That when I—*you*—woke, you'd go find her and get something to eat. Anyway, I fully deserve double helpings of algaecakes tonight, I think.

"Any luck in Saithe?" he asked. "Oh, and I heard the king coming back from his search just a while ago. But it didn't sound like him or his guards had made any progress finding Mala."

Ariel frowned, remembering what Karina had told her to do. She and her father were both still empty-handed, and they were running out of time.

"I'm going to talk to Father about everything I've found. I've got to tell him," Ariel said. *He is no closer to finding Mala than he was on my ceremony date. It's because he's so resistant to anyone's ideas but his. If we can put our fins together, we can find Mala faster, I'll bet.* "I need to be involved in the investigation! We all do."

Flounder wished her luck, and Ariel rehearsed everything she wanted to say before knocking on her father's door.

"Come in." King Triton sat on a shell throne on a raised dais in the sitting room adjacent his bedchambers, drowning in scrolls—maps marked with big red Xs. Names written on a *long* scroll lined the table that ran the breadth of his room, and most of them were crossed out.

"Father?"

He gazed up at her, and the lines in his face deepened.

"Ariel, you're feeling better? I heard you were sick." He rose, his eagerness matching the inflection in his voice. She was happy she could bring a smile to his face.

"Yes, much. I think I just needed rest."

"Well, good. Julia was worried."

"Yes, yes. I need to go see her once I leave here. I just wanted to talk to you." She rubbed her tail, fighting the urge to fidget.

Her father's jaw hardened. "Listen, if this is about how things went in High Sun, I know I shouldn't have yelled at you that way. There's no excuse for it, so I won't make one. We have no new leads on Mala. The others"—he sighed, eyeing the long list of names—"didn't pan out. But Usengu has some other ideas we're meeting about tonight once his rounds are done." His voice broke, and his wrists moved toward each other almost magnetically. He turned and rested his hands firmly on his hips instead. He wouldn't rub them together in front of her. He wouldn't show his sadness. As if that made him strong. But if Ariel had learned anything those past few days, it was that it took courage to face grief. Expressing his feelings made him strong.

She pulled on his hefty arms and turned him around. "I'm worried about her, too."

"Yes, of course." He cleared his throat. "What brings you here?"

The tightness in Ariel's chest squeezed. "So you're not going to be happy about what I'm going to say."

Was she really going to tell him everything? Admit how she'd defied him? Confess to him that she and Perla had almost been killed in Bone Reef? She tugged at her locs. She had to do this. Mala was out there somewhere, and Father didn't have half a clue how to find her.

His lips formed a thin line, but Ariel gulped down the lump in her throat. "I've been investigating what happened to Mala, too . . . behind your back."

"You *what*?" Anger cinched his brows.

"Stop!" Ariel raised her voice, and the king startled. It felt altogether foreign, but she'd gotten his attention. "Listen to me . . . please. You need to hear this."

Her father shook his head, already fuming, but he kept his mouth shut, which Ariel appreciated. And she told him everything: the note from Mala, the broken Safety Seal, their trip to Fracus and then to Bone Reef. "The short of it is, I think MerHunters are working with someone to hunt mermaids, because the spots on the map were areas merfolk frequent. They were scoping out Bone Reef! We've heard that tensions between the merfolk and Sea Monsters are at an all-time high. And Tolum, in Saithe . . ."

Her father's brow furrowed. She had his attention now.

"Tolum said that it isn't just Sea Monsters causing trouble, but apparently a mermaid is, too. There is too much happening for this all to be a coincidence. It has to do with Mala. And since the only ones who could break the palace seal in High Sun are you and the Residents, a Resident *must* be responsible." She tried to blow out a breath, but couldn't. She realized her hands were tightly linked together, nails digging into her skin.

She'd said it. It was all out there. She braced for his reaction, but for several moments her father said nothing.

The king swam away from her, his lips pinched in that way they did when he was thinking really deeply about things.

"Well?" she said.

"Tolum cannot lie. It's his gift. I gave it to him."

"Right." *Wow, is he really listening?*

"And you learned all of this by yourself?"

"Karina and Perla and I have been working on it," Ariel admitted.

"Together?" The king seemed surprised. "Karina and Perla? That is unlike them."

She nodded. "Karina and Perla have made amends."

Father's eyes widened. The words seemed to trigger a memory in him. He rose from his seat, and the hard lines on his face deepened. "They remind me of how I used to act with someone," he said, more to himself than to her, his gaze far off.

"They do?" He'd never mentioned anything of the sort before.

"I used to know a sea witch. We would bicker all the time, but we were close. But then she did something so terrible"—the king's jaw clenched—"she got banished."

"I had no idea." *Why hasn't he mentioned that before?* Ariel wouldn't press, not right now. Not until they found Mala.

"I don't know what to say about this information you've brought me, Ariel," he said, changing the subject. "I have to sit with this. But thank you. I'll weigh everything you've said. You have my word. You should know, though, that I've got good reason to think High Sun Sea Monsters are behind Mala's disappearance. They have been left unchecked for far too long."

"Father, not all Sea Monsters are untrustworthy just because we don't know much about them. Silius—"

"Do not lecture me on the dangers of seafolk in these waters, Ariel. I could tell you stories your grandpa told me that would leave you sleepless for years. And you said yourself that even you think a Resident must be involved."

"Still, Father. Are me and my sisters one and the same?" Ariel said. "Can you sum up a whole folk by the actions of one or two? Even if one of the Residents did take Mala, that doesn't mean all Sea Monsters are bad."

"Aren't you? Judging them all by Silius and Tolum's good nature?"

She sighed, exasperated. That was a battle she'd have to fight later. "Well, anyway, I want to be involved in the investigation from here on out. This happened in my sea, so I feel responsible." Her mother's face came to mind, the little she could remember of it. That wasn't entirely it, but those were the words she could admit aloud right now. She had her own struggles in the courage area. "I've shown you I can contribute valuable—"

"You're so much like your mother."

Her father's words stopped Ariel in her tracks.

"What?" She hadn't expected that. Father rarely spoke of Mother. Did he mean it? "I—I am?" How could she be like someone she hardly knew? Whose face she could hardly remember? She gazed down and realized she was stroking the purple pebble bracelet that hugged her wrist.

"It is my job to keep you all safe. Now Mala's gone. If your mother, the queen, who knew this ocean as well as I do, if not better, could get—" He held his mouth shut, as if not saying the words somehow made them hurt less. "*Please*, I beg you, stop looking for your sister on your own. Let me handle it, child." He pulled her into a hug. His wrists snapped together behind her back, but she could feel them rubbing together. Ariel allowed him hold her.

She remembered when Mother and Father both would put her to bed. They'd carry her together, her little self wedged between them in a sandwich hug all the way to her room. It was the only memory she had of them together. The rest had faded. She had been so small.

The king held up her arm, turning the bracelet around it. "You still wear it."

Ariel nodded. "You never told me where Mother got it from."

"Haven't I?"

"No." She settled in his arms, and a smile ghosted across his face.

"Your mother begged me to go out exploring—on expeditions, she'd call them. She loved seeing new places, discovering what wonders they held," her father said. "I hated it. I'll be honest. But she was stubborn, like you."

Ariel's cheeks burned, but she couldn't help smiling. Exploring? Her mother sounded so adventurous.

"So she pressed and pressed until I relented. The first time she went out, she agreed to take guards with her, and she found that purple pebble." He stroked her wrist. "She'd never seen one in that hue or shape, and she was just enamored. She collected all sorts of things, you know."

"She did?"

He nodded, and Ariel felt an odd tug in her stomach.

"That last morning when she was alive, she'd let you play with the pebble. When she didn't come back that day or the next, you clung to that thing. You wouldn't give it up. You refused to sleep or eat without it."

Ariel held rigidly still, afraid to move and miss a single breath of what her father was saying. Now that he'd opened this box, she burned with the need to look through it. The feeling confused her. She'd never mourned over Mother before . . . not like her sisters. Still, she held in a breath and hung on her father's words.

"I had it made into a bracelet for you so you could keep it close to you forever. That was the only thing that got you to sleep in those years. It was like a piece of her she left with you. And somehow you knew it."

She held her wrist to her chest. "The stuff she collected, where did it all go?"

He shook his head. "Every little bauble was a reminder of her absence. My failure to protect her. I couldn't bear the sight of it." He wasn't ready to face it. None of them were. "I got rid of it, foolishly thinking that would make it easier." He tapped his lip and gestured for her to follow. "You know, there was this one thing I kept."

He swam off, and Ariel stuck to his fins as he led her to a separate room that she realized must have been Mother's. Its shelves were empty, but the vanity where she'd gotten herself together was still covered in her jelly skin rubs and algae exfoliants. Untouched like a frozen memory. Her father reached under the vanity and pulled out a yellow box.

"What is it?" she asked.

King Triton opened the lid of the box, and a familiar sound filled the room. She gasped. The melody was one her mother hummed. Not a MerSong, but other tunes. She had loved music. Ariel twisted a dial on the box, and another melody played. It, too, was one Ariel recognized. Mother had insisted she and her sisters be trained in voice from when they'd been very little.

"Oh, Father!"

He pressed it into her hands. "It's yours."

"Really?"

"Really."

Ariel's cheeks pushed up under her eyes, and warmth flushed through her. For a moment she considered rubbing her wrists together, but the joy buzzing through her drowned any glint of sorrow. She had her mother's music box!

Knock. Knock. It was Usengu.

"Sire, Princess," he said in greeting.

"Usengu." Ariel put on her best smile as he squeezed her shoulder in sympathy.

"We're going to find her, sweet child."

She nodded.

"Now," her father chimed in. "Get to your room. Let me sit with all you've said."

"Thank you again, Father."

Ariel hugged the box to her chest all the way to her room. She'd failed to get Father fully on board. He was intent on being stubborn about letting her get involved in the investigation. But his resistance was rooted in fear. Grief. As it was for the rest of them.

And what about Mala? Would Father do all he'd said? Or dismiss it, thinking he knew best? Her father knew everything now, so he'd be watching her closely. She wasn't even sure she *could* sneak out anymore. Ariel sighed. What was she to do now?

Without any answers, she buried herself in her bed covers

and twisted the dial on the music box. She closed her eyes, imagining it was Mother singing to her.

And despite her worry, for the first time in a long time, for a reason she couldn't quite put into words—she fell into a deep, sweet sleep.

Chapter 13

One Day Until the Coral Moon

Ariel cracked the stalk of her samphire but could hardly hear its crunch over Indira and Caspia's chatter at breakfast. Julia, who still seemed noticeably shaken from Mala's disappearance, had let them know that their father had decided they could come out for meals, but he still expected them to stay in their rooms at all other times. Ariel chomped down on her food, thinking of Mala and all her father had said the night before.

The next day was the deadline to find Mala. Was Father going to give up his throne? The king hadn't publicized the ransom note to everyone in the castle, but from Julia's sour expression when she'd gotten Ariel up that morning and the downturned countenances of Father's guards posted around the room, it was clear some knew what was on the line.

Despite the glum mood, hushed anticipation for the Coral Moon Festival was on the lips of the servants as they moved about serving breakfast. But Ariel couldn't summon even a hint of excitement. The festival was a huge affair. It lasted from dawn to dusk, ending when the moon shone a vibrant shade of coral. Even the surface world seemed to celebrate, and colorful sparks would fly through the sky. Ariel and her whole household always watched the show from beneath the water. It was her favorite holiday. But this year it was something to dread, another reminder that those memories were fractured by her family in disarray, and that they were running out of time.

Ariel mulled over everything she knew about Mala, trying to fill in the holes. Had she missed something while in High Sun? Was there some tip about MerHunters she was overlooking? Should she head to the other territories and speak to the remaining Residents? Was there even time? She wasn't sure what the next best move was.

"Could you pass the seaweed?" Caspia asked.

Ariel handed her a shallow dish full of the bushy delicacy.

"Heard you up late talking to Father," Indira said, sliding some of the vegetable onto her own plate.

"You were eavesdropping?"

"Hardly. You're loud," Indira said with her usual squealing laugh. Ariel grimaced. Her sister's lighthearted demeanor when their sister was out there in the clutches of some vile culprit galled her. "I just wish you would drop this whole Mala thing and move on."

"Mala's still in danger," Ariel said. "I'm not going to just sit by and do nothing."

Caspia popped a bite into her mouth, rolling her eyes. "I'll be so glad once this ruse is over."

"Ruse? You can't be serious!" How could they think such a thing about Mala, of all people? They were just going to find *some*thing to nitpick. It was downright selfish. Maybe if they knew half of what she'd told Father, they would feel differently.

She huffed. *Doubt it.* She wouldn't waste her breath.

"I'm sure it's some sinister plan for Mala to get away with whatever her personal motives are," Indira continued. "We keep telling you she's not worthy of the pedestal you have her on."

Ariel rose from the table. "There's no proof of what you're saying! You just sound resentful and bitter."

"Bitter? Resentful?" Indira rose, too, her nostrils flaring. "You don't have any idea what it was like, always being in Mala's shadow!"

"The perfect daughter," Caspia snarled.

"Mother's *favorite*."

Caspia nodded. *"Mala.* The first to be deemed Protector of her very own territory. Mala. The one with the best marks. Julia even let her make up her own bed, because she said Mala could do it better than she could!"

Okay, that Ariel hadn't realized. Mala was perhaps the favorite daughter. Ariel had always been in awe of her. She wanted to *be* like her. The way Mala was doted on by all of court, the way the seafolk in Chaine praised her . . . She heard that they had even created an All Hail Protector Day to celebrate her great leadership. But she seemed so deserving of all the greatest things in the world. So this . . . this . . . Ariel cupped a hand over her mouth to contain her grief. The tidal wave would shatter the dam holding it together. Holding *her* together. She tried to think positive, but fighting back was easier.

"So that's what this is about? Jealousy?" Ariel folded her arms. Indira snapped her mouth closed and Ariel saw something in her sister's expression she'd never seen before when they discussed Mala: sadness.

"Mala is sneaky and cunning," Indira said with a shaky voice. "She snuck out. She flouted the rules. She was always getting what she wanted, whether by manipulating Father with that 'perfect' smile of hers or just doing it anyway and getting a slap on the wrist. You never saw it, obviously, because you were so young and stayed here with Father, but we did. And we're not risking our lives to play her games."

"I—" Ariel began.

"No, you listen, Ariel." Caspia wagged a finger at her. "You're always looking at the great stuff she's done. But have you ever considered that you're focusing on the wrong things?"

Focusing on the wrong things?! She was focusing on putting her family back together. That was the *most* important thing!

"What's this commotion?" Her father thundered in. His eyelids sagged despite his blunt tone. Had he slept at all? "Quiet it down this instant. I have an important update about . . ." He sighed. "About Mala."

Ariel's insides did cartwheels. She felt like her tail had gone out from under her. Leaning on the table was all she could do to keep herself upright. What was it? Was she okay? Were they too late? Had the kidnapper changed the terms? Shortened their window?

"It's come to my attention that MerHunters have discovered more of our communities outside of Fracus."

Indira gasped, and Ariel bit down on her lip.

"Our location is no longer secure, and, well . . . I may as well tell you all of it." Her father's face fell. Ariel sat up taller. Despite his insistence on keeping her away from the investigation, he had taken what she'd told him seriously, it seemed, and looked into it even further.

"Usengu, my guards, and I have concluded that the kidnappers intend to hand over Mala to MerHunters if my throne is not abdicated by the deadline they gave. I cannot give up the crown without risking even greater consequences to our waters," he went on. "It is no secret that MerHunters appear in Fracus during the Coral Moon Festival because it brings so many of us to the waters. So I expect that is where the handover will happen. We are considering trying to lure the kidnapper here or set a trap for them there. But it might be too big of a risk. We can't let them know we're on to them and give them time to amend their plans. Nothing is definitive yet, but I just wanted you to know I'm doing everything in my power to get Mala back."

Ariel shivered at her father's words. A part of her had always known that he wouldn't be able to risk abdicating the throne, even if it was Mala's life on the line. Tensions in the seas were high enough without losing their ruler. But to hear her father acknowledge the choice he had to make out loud made her heart ache.

"Oh, my god!" Caspia glanced at Ariel, who gazed back at her with her best petty *I told you so* glare.

That was why the timeline ended in one day . . . and now that it seemed like the MerHunters knew so much more about the geography of their seas, how would they even know which areas to avoid? Ariel felt the weight on her chest double. They were running out of time.

"What's your plan for the Residents, Father?" she asked. If he had taken her words about the MerHunters seriously and talked to his guards, then surely he was also investigating the Residents.

Her father's expression shifted.

"Father?"

"Ariel, I did as I've promised. I've thought on it, and Residents are Sea Monsters I've thoroughly vetted, deeming them worthy of our trust. If one of them were a traitor, I'd know it." He cleared his throat. "That's all I have."

"Seriously?" Ariel pushed up from the table.

But his expression darkened, and he didn't acknowledge her. "You all will stay here until the festival is over. And before you try to argue, this is an order. I'm not asking!" Her father stormed out as fast as he'd come.

Did he hear me?

So that was his plan? Hide them away, after she'd just told him everything? How was locking them all up the answer? Ariel deserved to be out there searching, too. Anger roiled through her. Pleading with him to see that was a lost cause.

They had one day left.

One!

One day before the kidnapper handed Mala over to the MerHunters and she was gone forever, like Mother. Ariel couldn't let that happen again. She wouldn't. If Father wasn't going to listen, and with Perla and Karina gone, she had only one choice—to continue investigating *herself*.

But where am I to start?

None of the clues Ariel had found seemed to have a logical next step. She pondered over the kelp she'd found outside Mala's window at her Protector palace in High Sun, still haunted by Indira's and Caspia's last words to her. She wasn't focusing on the wrong things. Her investigation had brought Perla and Karina back together. They probably didn't know that, but still. And it had also brought her Flounder. How dare they insinuate she was off track.

What precisely did the kelp say?

What could have saved Mother could save me, too.

She'd been hard pressed to figure out what had happened to Mala. But what if . . . Ariel sat up. What if she *was* focused on the wrong thing? What if figuring out what could have saved Mother's life was what she should have been focused on this entire time? Ariel knew very little of that morning besides what Father had told her the night before. Shouldn't someone have seen something? Who had seen Mother before she left for Fisher's Kitchen to explore? Maybe Julia would know? Besides Julia, who else—

Ariel gasped. The truth hit her like a fin slap.

The one person who had never even shown her face after the morning Mother died. The one who avoided the family at all costs. The one who was Protector over the very sea Mother had died in.

Her sister Tamika.

Ariel *had* to go talk to her. Could she know something? Was that why she was so standoffish? If Tamika did have any information, Ariel couldn't wait for her to speak up or come around. If she'd learned anything from helping Karina and Perla reconcile, it was that she should never wait to reach out to those she loved.

Chapter 14

One Day Until the Coral Moon

Ariel slipped a note to Karina and Perla with Father's news in the post before pulling Flounder into her room. She updated him on everything her father had said, and the fish's eyes grew wide. He started filling a bag with things, hardly paying attention as she finished her story.

"Did you hear me?" Ariel asked. "MerHunters might be in Fracus *tomorrow*, my father thinks—for Mala!"

"I heard you," he said, his back still turned, fiddling with something.

"Well?"

"I assume we're going off somewhere dangerous to risk getting ourselves killed, so I'm just getting myself ready to go."

"Wait, you'll come with me this time?" She swam up beside him, fighting the urge to pull him into a hug. She didn't want to go alone if she didn't have to.

Flounder finally faced her. "Staying back last time was okay but still terrifying. What would they have done if they'd burst in here and saw I was impersonating you? That father of yours has a temper." He shuddered. "I figure my best chance is sticking by you. At least then I can help you look out for things."

Ariel pulled him into a tight squeeze and swam in a circle. "Oh, Flounder! You're the best friend a mermaid could ask for. This means the world to me."

"So where to this time?" Flounder asked, eyeing their suspect list, which, thanks to her father's tightened security, had been re-scribbled on a bit of inconspicuous seaweed. Everyone was on such high alert that there was no way they could travel during the day. They'd have to move at night, while the castle was sleeping.

"I've asked Karina and Perla to meet me in Fracus."

Flounder swam backward as if her words had knocked the air out of his gills. "No, this is where I put my fin down, Ariel. MerHunters are coming in hours and you want to go to Fisher's Kitchen, where—"

"Not to where my Mother was taken," Ariel quickly clarified. "We're going to the palace in Fracus to see my sister, well below the surface. She's going to tell me everything she knows."

Flounder didn't say anything for several moments as he hooked her bag over his head. "I'm guessing she doesn't know you're coming."

"No."

"Is she friendly, at least?"

"Um . . . I'm not sure, actually." It had been so long. His lips twisted nervously.

"I'm hoping, with Perla and Karina's help, we'll be able to convince her to let us inside," Ariel said. "And talk for once."

Flounder wrung his fins. "I sure hope so. The only thing in Fracus scarier than Fisher's Kitchen is Fracus at night."

As Ariel used her FastFins to take her and Flounder to Fracus, she rolled her plan around in her head. They had been able to sneak out Ariel's bedroom window once the sun set and they were able to hide in the darkness. What was she going to say to Tamika? She hoped Karina and Perla would indeed meet her there. She could hear them both now, chastising her about venturing out yet again when it was even more dangerous. But this time she wasn't heading to some icy graveyard full of killer kelp. She was just trying to get into her sister's home. Surely that had to be different. Ariel didn't want to face Tamika alone for a reason she wasn't ready to put into words.

She and Tamika had been close before Mother died. Tamika had always been the one who would keep an eye on Ariel or take her to explore the castle's nooks and crannies. Then she'd just vanished without a word. For years Ariel had blamed herself, sure she must have done something to push Tamika away. But now that she was older and wiser, she knew that was silly. It wasn't her fault Tamika had run. Still, it hurt the same.

Fracus beyond their mother's memorial was entirely a mystery to Ariel. As they entered Tamika's territory, none of the paths looked the same. Her fins churned hard against her as she pushed herself to go as fast as she could. Fisher's Kitchen was a dot in the distance, and she huffed a breath in relief when they passed the turnoff for it.

Ariel swam swiftly until the mermaid-tail-shaped finial atop her sister's tower shone in the distance. Flounder was tucked tight into her kelp-woven bag. She hooked an arm under him, holding him tight to her chest as the water pushed hard against them.

"Almost there. You all right?"

Flounder nodded, unable to speak because of the fierce pressure of the water against their bodies.

Ariel slowed as she approached what should have been the foot of the castle. But Tamika's palace looked as if it'd been swallowed by a nest of thorned plants, all woven around one another. There was no clear entrance. The castle was set far back, judging by the tower protruding above the weeds in the distance. She couldn't even get close.

"Someone doesn't like visitors." Flounder glanced at her and gulped.

"There's got to be a break in here somewhere." Ariel swam around looking for an in.

"There." Flounder pointed, and Ariel spotted the tiny protrusion almost buried in the dirt. Upon closer inspection, Ariel realized it was a tunnel only wide enough for one of them to get through at a time. She peered inside but blinked at the darkness.

"Hello?" Her voice ricocheted off its stone interior. The tunnel was the only way in. Her nerves twisted. How far did it go? Why would Tamika live like this? She took one more look around for any sign of Perla or Karina, but there was none. Her heart sank. She had hoped they would be here when she arrived, and she didn't have time to wait for them.

"I guess I'm going to have to go in there myself. Can you stay out here and keep watch?"

He shook his head. "I have no way to warn you if something's coming."

"Yes, but I don't know what's on the other side of that tunnel, and I don't want you getting hurt. My sisters will probably be arriving soon, anyway." She didn't know for sure, but, boy, did she want to believe it, especially once she'd seen how clearly Tamika did not want visitors.

"She hides away as if—" But Flounder's words broke off.

Ariel didn't need him to finish. She knew what he was going to say. *She hides away as if she has something to hide.* Tolum's voice trickled through her memory. A mermaid and a sea creature were interrupting the balance of things, he'd said. Could Tamika have been whom he meant? No, it couldn't be one of her own sisters. *Shame on you,* she chastised herself for even thinking it.

"Fine, I'll wait here," Flounder agreed. "But if I hear anything, I am coming after you!"

She tried to relax once more, but it was pointless. It felt like a rock was sitting on her chest. She swam forward.

"Okay, I'll be back." *Hopefully.* Ariel wormed her way into the tunnel. Despite her petite frame, it was extremely difficult. Stone grazed her arms and she could have sworn she felt prickly thorns pushing through the walls of the tunnel, scratching her skin. When she came out the other side, she was covered in small scrapes. She turned to take in her sister's full estate.

It was rotund, with rising towers and a glass dome in the center. Weeds had grown around its facade and covered most of its big open windows. Most of Fracus was not green, but here it was like Tamika had planted a forest. Ariel squinted in the darkness. Someone could be peering through the overgrowth, *watching her*. Goose bumps skittered up her arms as she moved close to the door.

She rapped on it twice.

Nothing.

Silence.

She knocked again, this time a bit harder, and something coiled around her arm. She tugged, but the thorned branch dug into her skin. She yelped at the sight of red. Ariel pulled away, but another branch curled around her waist. Sharp prickles stung her all over as she looked for some glimpse of who was lassoing her into their clutches.

"Wait, stop!" The ropes of seaweed squeezed. She fought against her tethers until one broke, to her relief. She squinted but could see only shadows and shifts of the light. She wiggled in every direction, trying to pull another off her, but the thorns had her around her waist and each moment cut deeper into her skin. The ropes reminded her of the icy kelp in Saithe, but these didn't seem to halt their assault when she stilled. "I-I'm Princess Ariel, *sister* to your Protector!" she shouted at the door, hoping someone behind there could hear her. This was Tamika's palace; if there were dangerous plants assaulting visitors, she had to know about it, right? "Is anyone in there? Can you hear me? If—if you'll give her my name, she'll tell you she knows me!"

The slithering plant stopped.

"Who did you say you are?" A voice with a note of familiarity called out from behind the door.

"It—it's Ariel, the king's daughter. Princess and Protector-to-be in Carinae," Ariel managed, eyeing the plants hovering by her face warily. "I come with a message from the king."

"You've come? You've really come?" A familiar brown eye peered at her through a hole in the door.

"Tamika?"

The door slid open just a crack, enough that Ariel could make out who was behind it. She could hardly remember her sister's face. It had been so long, but she'd have known those brown eyes and curly dark brown hair anywhere.

"How do I know . . . you're alone?" Tamika asked.

"I'm alone, I swear." She held up her hands.

Something snapped behind her, a disturbance in the brush. Tamika opened the door wider, gazing out at whatever the ruckus was behind Ariel, and panic dented her brow.

"*Liar!* Tie her up and lock her in the dungeon!"

Ariel shook her head. She couldn't believe her ears. She looked behind her and realized the source of the disturbance: Karina and Perla had dislodged themselves from the tiny tunnel and were swimming toward them. They'd come!

"Tamika, it's me! A-and Perla and Karina. But no one else. I swear. Please!" Every word she yelled only deepened the knot in her stomach and tightened the thorns holding her chained. Her ribs ached; it felt like they were held together by a thread. The door swung open fully and Tamika moved aside to let out a critter with claws bigger than his body. He pulled at Ariel's thorned tethers, brushing them away. Then he secured her hands behind her back.

"Perla, Karina," she shouted. "Help!"

They rushed toward her, but the critter's claw smacked Perla in the face, knocking her down. Karina swam up, aiming a rock she held at the creature, but it gripped her by the tail and flung her to the side.

"No, don't hurt them—Tamika, *please!*" Ariel kicked and screamed, the urge to rub her wrists together biting at her.

"Protector's orders," the critter murmured to himself as he dragged Ariel inside with a monstrous strength that was entirely unexpected for his small size. After a few moments, Karina and Perla were bound as well. Ariel gazed at Tamika, blanketed in shadow, watching Ariel be pulled away. Tamika's skin was pallid and blotchy, and her lips arced down as if they were permanently hung that way.

"All in the same cell?" the crustacean asked.

Lines decorated Tamika's brow as she scowled at Ariel, who stared back, searching for some hint of the sister she knew. But she wasn't there. She peered harder and realized the strain in Tamika's eyes, the tilt in her lips, was not scorn, but a sign of fear. Tamika was terrified.

"Sister, I swear we come in peace," Ariel pleaded once more. "We're not here to hurt you."

Tamika raised a hand, and the clawed minion pulling Ariel by her wrists halted. She looked between them all before settling on Karina.

"No, look at me." Ariel knew Karina and Tamika's bitterness ran deep. "Tamika, it's me, Ariel. Remember, you used to read to me before bed."

"No . . . n-no." Tamika froze as if Ariel's words wore the face of a ghost. She squinted, then blinked. "My family may as well be dead."

Ariel gasped. Tamika's words were like barbed seaweed in her chest. Why would she say such a thing? Was that what had kept her away all those years? Sorrow hung on Ariel's shoulders, tugging her down like an anchor. "Tamika, I've missed you. Remember, I-I'd sneak into your bed at night because I was scared of those icky, slimy bedfish? And you'd hum Mother's songs to me?"

Tamika's eyes narrowed in disbelief. It had been so long since they'd seen each other, Ariel herself was probably hardly recognizable. Ariel wriggled, rubbing her wrists so hard she was shaking.

"Touch my hair," Ariel said. "Take my hand."

Tamika approached hesitantly and coiled Ariel's hair around her finger. Her lips parted, and breath caught in Ariel's chest. She was listening.

"Truly," she breathed. "We are here in peace."

Tamika's fingertips traced the curves of Ariel's face. Her lips flinched as her mouth puckered in sorrow. Tamika swallowed, nodding, and pulled her into a hug. "Oh, Riri. I am so sorry."

The cinch in Ariel broke. *She believes me.* Tamika gestured at the clawed creature, and Ariel felt her wrists release. Ariel squeezed her sister again in relief. "Now, please, Tamika, there isn't much time. Untie us. We have much to tell you."

Chapter 15

One Day Until the Coral Moon

Tamika's palace was as quiet as a graveyard as she led them through the foyer into a sitting room. There were no living things around, aside from her clawed creatures. Noigets, she'd called them—Sea Monsters that Tamika had apparently taken under her wing and into her castle, then armed thoroughly to ensure her fortress wasn't penetrated. Ariel had never heard of anyone working with Sea Monsters who weren't Residents before. The thought tugged at her lips and filled her with warmth.

"Let me grab some salve for those cuts." Tamika disappeared.

"Thank you so much for coming," Ariel said to Karina and Perla. "I wasn't sure what to expect, since, you know . . . I told you I'd try to stay out of trouble."

"Yeah, well, I said I'd be there for you. And I meant it." Karina squeezed her arm as Tamika returned.

"Here we are. Sorry about all the security . . . my home has to be safe," Tamika said, trying to explain as she rubbed lotion onto Ariel's cuts. "I don't allow visitors here. Especially with the tensions I've been hearing about here in Fracus."

"We can tell," Perla said, rubbing her own wrists, still sore from the restraints. "We met your Resident, Silius, and he had the kindest things to say about you. He also said that he desired an audience with you sometime."

"Oh, Silius. Sweet Silius," Tamika muttered under her breath. "How will he ever forgive me?"

"Why do you live like this?" asked Karina. "What happened—"

"What do you mean, what happened? You know what happened!" Tamika's hands shook, and Ariel closed her own around Tamika's, hoping it would calm her.

"Mother," Ariel whispered.

Tamika took a sharp breath. "Yes, Mother." Her words were barely audible. As if saying them made them hurt all the more. Ariel tried to read her sister. For the moment, she was grateful to not be on her way to the dungeon. But she had to get answers out of Tamika. Only she wasn't sure how.

"We're here because Mala's missing, Tamika," Ariel said. She softened her tone to try to ease the bombarding question. "Do you know anything about that?"

"Mala." Tamika scowled, snatching her hand away from Ariel. Karina and Perla exchanged a nervous glance.

"Annoyingly brilliant," Tamika said as she put distance between them, talking more to herself than anyone. "Polished and poised. Precious Mala. Frustratingly good at everything. The envy of the entire sea. *My* sister." Her lips curled; lines creased around her eyes. Ariel peered, hoping that smile was in pride . . . not jealousy. Tamika turned to them, and Ariel stayed frozen, waiting for Tamika to make her full feelings of Mala's being missing known.

"What sort of monster would do such a thing?" she said, her countenance stained with blatant shock.

"We don't know," Perla said.

"We're trying to figure that out." Ariel pulled the scribbled kelp from her bag. "She left us this note."

Tamika read it and paced, not entirely convinced. Ariel needed to tell her . . . everything. "And there's more." She and Perla detailed the whole account of the ransom note, and the visits to the memorial, Fracus, and Saithe. Everything she'd told Father, and his dismissive response. Karina updated them on the investigation in Saithe over her break-in.

Once they were done, Tamika swallowed and hung her head. "I should probably tell you about the morning Mother left."

Ariel and her other sisters shared a look.

"Only if you're ready to talk about it," Ariel said.

"If we're going to save Mala's life, it sounds like I have no choice." Tamika gestured for them to sit and had one of her nicer clawed friends bring them refreshments. The three of them settled onto her immaculate furniture, eager to soak in her every word.

"Everyone was staying at Father's palace. You'd all gone gathering shells that morning. Everyone but me and Riri. I wasn't feeling well, and to be honest, outings weren't ever fun when Mala and Indira and Caspia were there. The bickering was a constant headache. So I stayed and told Julia I'd keep an eye on you." She pointed at Ariel. "Well, Mother burst in my room a short while later, saying that she'd just heard that the spot where you all were swimming—Fisher's Kitchen—was being scoped by MerHunters that very day. You all were in grave danger." Tamika pulled at her throat. She shook her head. "I was so scared." Her voice cracked. "She told you and me to stay locked in our rooms until she or Father came to get us. But she never came."

Tamika curled in on herself. "By dinner I'd heard that Mother had been—" But her words broke off, and she turned her head away. "Later, I found out that you all weren't swimming at Fisher's Kitchen at all. You'd actually spent the day at Lily's Reef, on the complete other side of the sea. So I checked the logs, and we had no unusual visitors that day. The only random visitor in the castle that morning was Ursula the sea witch."

Ariel wrinkled her brow. Her father had mentioned a sea witch to her. She must not have come around often, because Ariel would have remembered her name, at least. She couldn't even picture her face.

"And did Ursula know anything?"

"You misunderstand me." Tamika choked on her next words, her lip trembling. She swallowed. "Ursula was the one to tell Mother you were in danger. *Don't you see?*" She turned to them, her eyes burning red with furious grief. "Mother was lied to! Led there by someone our family trusted, to be *killed!*"

Karina's and Perla's mouths fell open. The world swayed. Was that why Father had said what he said about Ursula? Why hadn't he told any of them the full story? Shouldn't they know if there was someone dangerous out to get their family?

Tamika inhaled. "Once I realized someone so close to Father couldn't be trusted, the palace felt unsafe. I left for

Fracus and never looked back. It was selfish, I know. I was just . . . so scared. I'm still . . ."

Ariel shuddered in horror before grabbing Tamika's hands, hoping she could feel her love and support. How terrifying it must have been, knowing that all these years. *Wait.* "Could Ursula be who is after Mala?"

"No, she was banished by Father with his trident's magic. She can't enter the kingdom," Tamika said. "No one has seen her for years."

Tamika's words rang with disappointment. Ariel was no closer to figuring out who had taken Mala. They were at a dead end. Her shoulders slumped as Perla swam closer, rubbing Tamika's back.

Karina brushed a hair out of Tamika's face. "Keeping all this bottled up like that was eating you up from the inside out, Mika."

So much pain strained Tamika's worn expression. Like so many of them, she was trying to tote this bag of grief over Mother. Ariel scooted closer to Tamika. Dead end or not, being there for Tamika made this whole trip worth it. Mother's loss had shredded them. They were fractured and broken, like a clam without a shell, floundering, looking for a way to piece their lives back together. How could Ariel make her see that only with all their arms could they shoulder it?

"Thank you for coming here. I-I'm sorry I almost threw you

in the dungeon." Tamika held her face. "I'm so embarrassed."

"Hey, almost getting killed is sort of my thing at this point," Ariel said. "So we're all good."

They all laughed, and Tamika's eyes creased at the corners. "I mean it, Riri. Thank you. Thank you so much. You will save more than Mala's life by coming here today."

"You were never meant to carry all this on your own. Mother gave us to each other." Ariel squeezed her sister's hand, and Perla and Karina piled their hands on top.

"Family," they said.

"Family," Tamika echoed.

They squeezed together in a hug, but Ariel's mind was still whirring at the dead end they were now at. *What could have saved Mother could save me, too.* It just made no sense. Ariel bit her lip. Her best bet was to go back to the drawing board, to the only clue she knew she could count on—that a Resident had broken that Safety Seal. They'd ruled out a few, but there were still some left. Time was running out.

Leaving Tamika in Fracus was difficult, but she wasn't ready to come back to the castle. Mending things with three of her sisters was as big of a step as she was ready to take. And even that had left her exhausted. She retired to bed before Ariel, Karina, and Perla went off, but not before warning them *again* of the growing tensions she'd been hearing of as the rumors about Father continued to spread. Ariel assured her that though she'd been hearing things, too, none of it was true as far as she knew. She wasn't sure who was spreading such rumors, but it wasn't helping, that was for sure.

Flounder had fallen asleep outside the tunnel during his watch, and Ariel was just relieved he was okay. Karina and Perla insisted on coming back to their father's palace. Her head hurt more the more she thought about Mother's death. There was no time to puzzle out Mala's cryptic message. She'd save her life and then ask her what it had meant.

"Well." Karina swam up beside her. "What are we going to do?"

"You mean you're not going to tell me to go to my room and hide and let Father fix it?" Ariel hadn't meant it to come out as snippy as it did.

"Uh, as if you'd listen. Clearly you aren't." Karina nudged her with her elbow, playfully. "No, but really, Perla and I have been talking about it, and you don't need us bossing you around. Look what you've done. I'm Protector over my own territory, and I haven't even managed to do this. You're getting us closer to Mala; you've got Tamika talking to us again."

The king's palace came into view and they picked up their swimming pace, Ariel detouring away from the castle toward her hideaway.

"What she's trying to say is," Perla cut in, "we're here for whatever you come up with next, Ari. We're following your lead."

Ariel must not have been hearing correctly. "You guys, seriously?"

"Yes. So what's the plan?"

What *were* they going to do? They were stumped. Stuck. With a list of Resident suspects and no idea which direction to head in. They'd wasted so much time on Mala's cryptic note, which had led nowhere helpful for finding their sister.

They arrived at the grotto to look over all they'd discovered the past few days to see if there was any indication of a Resident acting seedy or suspicious. Whoever it was had held this secret for many years, so maybe their ill will toward her family had shown somehow? Ariel paced as her sisters and Flounder picked over the nets she'd found, the scrap from the map, and the other odds and ends filling the shelves in her cavernous hideaway. They'd have to get back soon, and Karina and Perla would have to explain their sudden visit to their father.

Ariel mulled over what they knew, combing through every piece of information. Father only had Residents invited on special occasions or for interrogations. Could she ask Usengu? This would have happened under his nose! Father was particular about who was trustworthy and who wasn't.

What would he say when he learned how wrong he'd been? About so many things.

"Wait a minute." It was Flounder, holding up the sea kelp Mala had written her message on. "This isn't Carinaean."

"Huh?" Ariel asked, turning away from the piece of the map she had been inspecting. Karina and Perla also stopped what they were doing to glance at Flounder.

"This kelp. Look at it, its fibers are tough. It's leafy and thick. And it's light yellow on one side and a blue-green on the other," Flounder said. "This isn't a kelp that grows in the high-sun side of Carinae."

"What does that matter?" Karina pressed. "I don't get it."

Ariel frowned, replaying Flounder's words. If the kelp wasn't Carinaean, then it had to have been taken there. She studied Mala's loopy handwriting. *Why would she have kelp not from Carinae?* Then a new thought occurred to her. She had always imagined that Mala had written the note in a hurry, to give them a hasty clue in the wake of her attack. But what if the note wasn't from Mala at all? The note had spurred them in an investigation to look deeper into Mother's death. *What if . . .*

"What if that note was brought to High Sun and left by her kidnapper to throw us off track?" Ariel asked.

"In Mala's hand?" Karina asked.

"Maybe they forced her to write it?" *How could I not have thought of this before?*

Karina gasped. "You think? I mean, it's certainly been distracting."

"Could someone else have brought it with them?" Perla asked.

"But why in the ocean would anyone travel with kelp?" Ariel asked. It grew abundantly everywhere.

"They wouldn't," they all said at the same time. There was no plausible explanation other than its being planted to mislead them.

"Well, wait, if the kidnapper planted it, then where does that kelp grow?" Perla asked. "Would that tell us who wrote it? Wouldn't it help us figure out which Resident is our kidnapper?"

Whoever wanted to mislead them was either the kidnapper or involved somehow.

"Flounder, help me," Ariel said, two swishes ahead of her sister. "Those bound scrolls Julia gave me, where are they?"

Flounder handed her the scrolls, and she ripped through the pages. There was a section with seaweed from all over the ocean.

Perla shoved a nail between her teeth. Karina wrapped her arms around herself, waiting with bated breath. Ariel flipped and flipped, sifting through hundreds of pictures until she spotted what she was looking for. There in the center of the page was a picture almost identical to the kelp the message had been written on. Her finger raced under the words.

Clumilia seaweed is a unique flora species . . .

Found only in one part of the ocean . . .

She gasped.

"Which sea is it?" Flounder hooked his fins, shifting nervously.

She blinked and read the page again to be sure. How could that be? But there it was in squid ink.

"This kelp is only found in the Chaine Sea," Ariel said.

"What?"

"You mean . . ."

"Yes." She glanced at the kelp again. "The Resident from Mala's own territory must have penned that note."

Chapter 16

One Day Until the Coral Moon

Perla and Karina scrubbed the shock from their faces.

"Should we get back to the palace?" Perla asked. "Before they notice you're gone?"

"I need a little more time to think," Ariel said, turning the scroll over and over in her hands.

"You both go and distract Father with some reason why you've come in so late. Flounder and I are going to figure out what to do next." Ariel already knew what she needed to do, but there was no way Perla and Karina would go for it. She wasn't even sure Flounder would.

"All right, but hurry. Ariel, I'm scared," Perla said.

Perla and Karina hugged her goodbye as Flounder swam back and forth, tapping his lip.

"So wait," Flounder said. "What about what Tolum said? A mermaid and a monster upsetting things? What did that mean?"

"I don't know." It didn't make sense.

"Maybe there is a mermaid in Chaine that's jealous of Mala?" Flounder said.

That would seem more likely with what Tolum had said, but Ariel couldn't make much sense of that, either. "Mala is so loved there. So very loved. It's hard to imagine. Are we sure Tolum knows for sure a mermaid is involved?"

"Not exactly. He can't lie. But that's not the same thing as what he said being true," Flounder said. "His exact words were that he *heard* a mermaid is involved. So all we know is that he did in fact hear that rumor."

"Hmmm, so it could be nothing more than a rumor." Her head throbbed at the what-ifs. Time was ticking. "I have to go to Chaine, Flounder. I need to see what's going on for myself."

Flounder shook his head, backing away. Ieka wasn't just any Resident. He was the notorious venomous creature of Chaine. Half sea snake and half barracuda, and the first Resident to ever be designated because Father wanted *him* most of all kept on a leash. His kind were deadly predators with night vision and sound cloaking, so no one could hear them coming.

"They're capable of *atrocities*," her sisters had told her Father had explained when he refused to let any of them participate directly in the Chaine Resident ceremony. Ariel didn't have to ask Flounder or her sisters or anyone how they'd feel about the idea of her going to Chaine.

"Remind me, what is Ieka's gift?" Ariel asked.

Flounder grimaced.

"Tell me."

"He can paralyze his prey with just a look. B-but it makes him a little weaker every time he uses it."

A shiver went up Ariel's spine. "You head back to the palace. I already have my Fins, so I'm going to get there now. We don't have time to waste. I need you to keep an eye on any other suspicious activity in and out of here."

"You don't want me to come?" He narrowed his eyes.

"I just wanted to make sure someone knew the plan in case . . . in case I don't come back. And—" She was the worst liar. "Okay, and maybe I'm a wee bit concerned about Ieka. And I don't want you getting hurt. But I'm going to be fine, I'm almost sure."

"Almost, huh?"

"Those are really the best odds we could hope for."

His head hung. "Please be careful, Ariel. You're the only family I've got."

"I will." Ariel squeezed Flounder in a hug before they said their goodbyes.

Outside the grotto, it was the dead of night—technically early morning. With no one in sight, Ariel blew out a huge breath. She hoped she was doing the right thing. She could see no other option. But at least she wouldn't be putting anyone else she cared about in danger with her.

She checked the latch on her FastFins with shaky hands. This was the key to finding Mala, she knew. She just hoped going there alone wasn't stupid. She would scope out the place and look for some sign that Mala was being held there. If she got a whiff that she was right, she'd grab Father and his guards. If she saw Mala with her own eyes, he wouldn't be able to argue with that.

Her gut had led her right thus far. *Please let me be right about this.* She clutched the pebble Mother had given her on her wrist and took off.

The Chaine Sea was cooler than Fracus and not nearly as creepy as Saithe, but Ariel swam cautiously, keeping an eye out. The moon glowed on the water's surface above her, and she stuck close to the top of the sea for better visibility.

Chaine wasn't brightly colored like the high-sun side of Carinae or dark and cold like Saithe. Nor was it mountainous like Fracus. But there was something distinct about it. It was like a jungle underwater. The whole ocean was rich with greenery, more than she'd ever seen; kelp, seaweed, and all other kinds of thick bushy plants with narrow waxy leaves. Even the flowers on them were green.

Ariel stopped when she spotted a stone statue in the shape of a mermaid. She'd almost thought it was Mother's local memorial until she studied it closer. There was no crown on her head or fancily shaped jewels wrapped around her arms and neck, and instead of having her mother's natural curls, this mermaid's hair was bone straight. They'd made a monument of her sister? Tiny letters inscribed on the bottom confirmed her suspicions.

In Honor of Our Beloved Princess Mala, it read. Ariel smiled, touching the statue's face. *We're going to find you, sister.* Beside the statue was a sign with arrows pointing in every direction. She skimmed them until she found the one she was looking for.

CHAINE FALLS

Ieka would likely be near the underground waterfall. Before they parted, Flounder had told her that Ieka's kind thrived in rushes of moving water. On occasion they'd stick their heads above the water, and the curtain of a waterfall was the perfect cover for a creature like him to hide. Ariel unclenched her fists and swam in that direction.

Rocks piled higher around her the farther she went. The foliage grew more sparse, shifting to shallow beds of lime-colored coral and fish in all shades of green, so camouflaged they were hard to see. Water rushed around her; the top of Chaine Falls didn't even break the water's surface. She stilled, gaping at its beauty. She'd never seen a waterfall before, and it was more glorious than anything she could have imagined. No wonder Mala loved it here. The seafolk adored her, and it was certainly easy on the eyes.

Ariel swam deeper, further into the falls, between dips and craters, looking for a way to get behind the curtain of water. Underground waterfalls were tricky. You had to find the center of the plunge pool and dash beneath. She spotted the thickest sheet of water and braced herself before dashing through. Water beat against her head, rattling her insides like a drum. She hurried until the drumming stopped, the overhang of water was behind her, and cavernous rock surrounded her.

"Ooooo."

Ariel stilled.

"Ooooooo. Arrrggggh."

"Hello?" Chills ran up her arm as she looked for the source of the sound. Wailing flitted through the water again. She followed it, and the cave opened up even wider. She spotted a long pointed tail and followed it to the body and head of a *massive* creature she'd seen once before. She sucked in a breath.

Ieka.

She'd wandered right into his den! He was silver and long, his tail curled like a snake and finned like a shark. Her blood turned to ice as he turned and met her eyes, apparently sensing her presence.

Ariel looked around for some sign of Mala but came up empty. She told herself to move, to say something, but her tail and mouth didn't obey. His eyes glinted at her, and she backed up right into a rocky wall. There was nowhere to go. *Does he have my sister? Is she here?*

She needed to be brave.

"H-hello. I-I'm Princess Ariel, daughter to the king and Protector Princess Mala's sister. I've come to find out where you're keeping her. We demand she be returned immediately." She froze, waiting for his response, hoping that the green in his eyes didn't mean what she feared it meant. His lips were thin and pulled back, showing his rows of razor teeth. She tried hard not to look at them.

Ieka stared at her a moment longer before his eyelids

drooped, his lips sagged, and he turned away, groaning again. Ariel's brows kissed. She'd just accused him of holding the princess. He wasn't going to respond? Was he going to attack her? She gulped down her nerves and swam toward him.

"Ieka?"

He wailed again. If there had been words in there, she couldn't make them out. Ariel swam closer and noticed nets wrapped around his pectoral fin.

"Oh, my goodness." That wailing she'd heard was *pain*? "These are hurting you."

The Sea Monster nodded, and she spotted the thinnest thread tied tight around his mouth, keeping his jaw shut. He couldn't talk. He could only moan. *Who would do such a thing?* Was she wrong? Perhaps she didn't know the full story. If Ieka was Mala's kidnapper, why would he be bound here like this? Her hands worked furiously, undoing the ropes that bound him. The knots were stubborn, but she worked at them until they came begrudgingly undone. If she hadn't come along, there was no way he could have gotten himself out of that without thumbs. She tugged on the last restraint, and it broke.

Did he have Mala? It certainly didn't seem like it. If anything, it seemed like he was a prisoner, too. Did he know something? That kelp with the note on it had come from this sea, and he was the only one in Chaine who could have fiddled with the Safety Seal. Was Flounder right, and some other local mermaid was involved?

"Thank you, Princess." Freed, Ieka spun in a circle, flexing his fins. He shook, and Ariel could have sworn she heard the cave around them shift.

She straightened. "You're welcome."

His giant head drooped, entirely disarming. Ariel moved closer for a better look behind him. But there was only barnacled rock and clustered plants. No tied-up mermaid or even a sign of one. She couldn't figure out quite how to read him. *Was he involved? Should I be scared? Have I made a mistake letting him go?*

Finally she asked, "How long have you been here like this? Who did this to you?"

"I know exactly why you're here, Princess." His voice was low, sponged with age and a weariness Ariel didn't quite understand. He pulled a necklace from a hook wedged in the rock and stroked it, doting on the charm before dragging himself back over to her languidly. "The waters talk. They've told me Mala's been kidnapped."

He knows. She narrowed her eyes. Maybe he had nothing to do with it at all? But the kelp and the seal . . .

"I need you to tell me what you know about Mala's

disappearance. I have reason to believe that you fiddled with the Safety Seal around the Carinaean palace, as it is within your authority to do so, and have taken her . . . against . . . her will." But the more she spoke, the more uneasy she felt. Her words didn't move him. He only turned the necklace in his fins. He was so sad and lethargic. *Could he really be a kidnapper? Or even an accomplice?*

This moment felt eerily familiar. She'd been in this place before, expecting the worst of a Sea Monster because that was the norm. But her gut didn't lie, and at the moment it was telling her Ieka wasn't a threat. That didn't mean he didn't know anything, though. Accusing him, however, judging him, wasn't going to be productive. She settled on a rock beside him. "O-or anything you might know that could be helpful," she added, her tone softening. "I'll hear it."

"I just miss her, you know?"

Wait. "Mala? You're upset about Mala?"

"I'm a sap, I know. Not what you were expecting, I suppose. I usually try to do a good standoff just to give folks a show, but . . . these days . . ." His head hung. "I just can't hide what I am feeling."

Ariel shook her head, trying to fully digest what he was saying. He missed her. Like, *missed* missed her? She was Protector there, so Ariel guessed that made sense. *He can't be her kidnapper.* Ariel mentally crossed him off her list.

"She used to do this thing, you know, where she'd smile and . . . and these little craters would form in those puffy things on your face."

"Cheeks?"

"Cheeks, yes." His lips split in an even wider smile, and it was entirely terrifying to watch him bare more of his teeth. But the lines hugging his eyes flickered with a warmth that hadn't been there a moment earlier. Ariel couldn't believe her ears or her eyes at this point. The world wasn't spinning, but Ariel could have sworn it was. Ieka . . . this creature . . . the fearsome monster . . . he . . .

"You love my sister."

"That obvious, huh?"

"Do the Chaine seafolk know?"

"The gossip travels fast. Some might, I'm sure."

Questions, so many questions, but Ieka had settled on the rock against her, a slight smirk on his face as he reminisced. "I told her people would find out. That we should do it the right way and appeal to the king. But she told me that would be wasted effort."

Do it the right way?

"We just wanted to be together, you know? Gosh, it feels so good to just *tell* someone."

Be together? As in . . . Ariel sat up. Was he saying what she thought he was saying?

"Wait, what exactly are you getting at?"

"Mala and I, we . . . we eloped."

Ariel braced herself against the rock at her back. *A monster and a mermaid would protect each of the seven seas, forbidden to love, forbidden to flee.* She dug her hands into the roots of her hair. What was he saying? What had they done? *The rules of our world are being tested. A mermaid and a Sea Monster are upsetting the balance.* Ariel gripped the rock beneath her just to be sure she wasn't floating. Tolum's words suddenly made sense.

"We planned to keep it a secret, Princess, really. We just didn't see any reason we shouldn't be allowed to pair up formally. The king—"

"I quite agree," Ariel said.

"Wait, you do?"

"I do." Ariel couldn't think of a single reason the Treaty made sense. And even more so now from what she'd seen with her own eyes the past several days. Father would write her off as naive, but he was being narrow-minded! There was no way the Residents were the only trustworthy Sea Monsters in the sea. And if her sister was in love with Ieka, or *anyone*, she couldn't see why they shouldn't be allowed to be together. It was unreasonable. The Treaty was archaic, enforced by Father but founded by his ancestors. They'd crafted it out of fear, wanting to keep Sea Monsters and others apart. But Father was in charge now, and he must see there was no reason for such unjustness.

"Who knows?" Ariel asked.

"No one's supposed to."

"Oh, Father . . . when he finds out . . ."

He would blow his top over this. Her sister had married her Resident in secret! *Married* him. But that was all tangential to the matter at hand. She had to find Mala first. She picked through the bits and pieces of all she knew. Something still wasn't fusing together. That kelp had come from Chaine, but her seafolk loved her. Her Resident was the only one there who could have broken the seal. She dug her fingers into her temples. *Think!*

"I was just trying to protect her," Ieka said. He shook his head mournfully. "Can't you see?"

His voice cracked, and Ariel scooted closer to the massive animal and tried to stroke his fin in comfort. "I didn't know he would trick me!"

Wait . . . "Who—"

"I didn't know once I did what he said"—his voice rose, thundering in the rocky dwelling—"he'd bind me up and swim off and steal her."

"Who is *he*?"

But Ieka left her side to dig through a pile of brush wedged between two rocks. He plucked out something and handed it to Ariel. A piece of seaweed exactly like the one Mala had written a message on.

"So it *was* you? You wrote the message."

"I didn't know what it was for. I'd gone to him to talk to him about us, hoping there was a way we wouldn't have to live in hiding. I trusted him. But he turned on me, chastising me for breaking such a sacred rule. Then he promised he would keep our secret from the king if I wrote this message on a piece of kelp for him in Mala's handwriting. We have worked together so long; I know it by heart. So I did as he asked, and that's when he hinted that he had seedy motives. I reached for my gift right then, but he held up a shiny glass, and it paralyzed *me* instead. Then he bound me up while I was weakened. By the time the paralysis wore off, he was long gone." His giant shoulders shook, and Ariel couldn't get a word in edgewise. "Eventually some seafolk came by. They couldn't untie me and promised to get help, but never returned. But while they were here they did tell me the grave news about her. I—I felt so bad. So responsible. Somehow my note was her undoing. He used me to hurt her, and I can never forgive myself—"

"Wait, wait. Slow down. *Who* tricked you? Who did all this?"

He met her eyes. "The king's right hand—Usengu."

Chapter 17

One Day Until the Coral Moon

*U*sengu?

The world tipped sideways, and Ariel felt it all over her skin. She closed her eyes in case that would help things stop spinning.

"I don't understand," she finally managed to say. "Usengu's known me since I was a fry. You're saying he kidnapped Mala?"

"I'm sorry to be the bearer of bad news, Princess," Ieka said.

Ariel couldn't move, frozen by shock.

"Usengu has only ever been loyal to the king, a devout

trident-follower," Ieka continued. "To be honest, when he had me write the note, I didn't really understand it. It didn't seem sinister, exactly. Maybe it was a game or jest. I wasn't sure. All he'd said was some friends of his needed a history lesson. I was naive, I realize in hindsight."

"Usengu? Overseer of Residents? Sea serpent with the dark green tail and yellow spots?"

"Yes, Princess."

Ariel shook her head, got up, and paced. She couldn't believe her ears. Usengu was one of her father's trusted few. Usengu had been at her ceremony in Carinae. He was helping Father *lead* the investigation to find her sister. Between meetings, he was tirelessly traveling territory to territory, supposedly looking for whispers on what had happened to Mala. Was it all a cover? Lies? Or was Ieka lying?

"Please don't take this the wrong way," Ariel said, eyeing the Sea Monster carefully for any sign of deceit. "But do you have proof?"

Ieka gave Ariel a stack of seaweed just like the kind Mala's supposed note was written on. These bore a similar message in the same slanted handwriting as the one she'd found outside Mala's window.

"I don't understand," Ariel said.

"He had me write it a few times until it sounded the way he liked. He didn't dispose of them well." Ieka peered closer at the kelp. "You can see here, those finprints aren't mine."

Ariel peered at the spot he was looking at, and sure enough, she could see that the smudges she had noticed on the kelp earlier were actually tiny imprints where someone with smaller fins had held it.

He held up his big fins. "They are way too small to be mine. If you could check them with Usengu's, they'd match."

She bit her lip. Finprints were unique to the creature. And these certainly were not Ieka's. The pressure in the cave squeezed her chest. "I recognize the grime. Usengu's always wiping his slimy fins on things." How had she not noticed earlier? The random marks on the kelp weren't random marks at all.

Had Usengu really done this? She stilled with shock. Usengu bolstered Father's distrust of other creatures with tales about how so many of the ones he'd met on his travels to the territories were untrustworthy. He was always insisting to Father that one had to be careful whom one trusted. Had he fed Father's fear only to try to exploit it? Ariel felt sick.

"I don't know what to say." She didn't. But she knew what to do. She had to tell her father, but carefully. He was hard to dissuade, and she knew that his trust in Usengu ran deep, but the evidence Ieka had given her should help.

"What else can you tell me?" Ariel asked.

"My best guess is that Usengu's been stirring up tensions,

sowing discord in the territories to make a move for Triton's throne. He has many who are loyal to him, and with the lies being spread about the king, they may be willing to do anything to help Usengu."

The ransom note. Any one of his followers could have sent it if that were true. Perhaps that was why Father's lead on who'd written the ransom note had gone nowhere. Usengu was everywhere, and yet he was nowhere. He kept his fins clean.

"I suspect he may have told some our secret, because I'd heard whispers about animosity building against mermaids in Chaine. A lot of my kind don't like to see a union between us," Ieka said. "They think of the Princess Mala as some fancy royal with no concern for regular folks. They think she's hoodwinked me into this flagrant disregard of the rules, I guess. And the merfolk assume, I would imagine, that I manipulated Mala or something ridiculous. It's a mess on both sides."

Ariel's thoughts tossed like a wave on a stormy sea. But she could see clearly, finally. If what Ieka said was true, Usengu was stirring up the discontent with the king, and painting mermaids as manipulative and contentious. And of course the ocean was ripe for it; look how her father ostracized Sea Monsters. This was a disaster, and King Triton wasn't exactly innocent.

Anger burned in her, and the discomfort that had sprouted in her days ago grew into full bloom. Father's scoffing over the years about Sea Monsters had cemented a perception of them in all her sisters' minds and at court. It had eroded, little by little, the sense that they deserved to be treated with respect and judged by their own merits. Even her own nerves at meeting Ieka, the shock of Silius's and Tolum's being so unlike anything she'd been taught they would be . . . She felt sick. The disdain for Sea Monsters, the assumed superiority of merfolk was spreading like an infectious algae. And it was killing people. It was about to kill her sister!

The pieces fell into place. Usengu certainly had access. He could travel as the king did; he was Father's right hand. He very well could have broken the seal to frame a Resident. Now that she thought of it, he hadn't been around when Mala turned up missing. Father and his guards had gone into meetings, which always included Usengu, so she'd assumed he was in them. But she hadn't seen him with her own eyes. And she seemed to recall Father saying *"find* Usengu," she realized. She steadied herself on a wall. *Oh, my goodness.* Usengu . . . how had she not seen it all along? "I'm so sorry," Ariel said.

Ieka lifted his head, his eyes wide with surprise. "Wait, you believe me?"

"I don't feel good about anything you've said, but I can

see you're honest." Ariel offered him a fin shake. "Thank you for trusting me with all you've told me. *I* won't betray you."

"Mala was right. You are so much like the queen. I didn't know her personally, but from everything Mala's told me. Your heart; your fiery, determined spirit."

Ariel warmed all over. Her mother had always been an enigma to her. But Ieka's words made her feel close to her, as if pieces of her mother were woven in every fiber of her. *Could I actually be like Mother? Everyone else sure seems to think so.* Ariel's wrists pulled toward each other in a rush of emotion, and it caught her off guard. This was about finding Mala. Not about Mother.

But . . . maybe it was always about Mother.

For Tamika it had been. Karina and Perla's bickering, too. Indira and Caspia were bitter, no doubt because they were tortured by a grief they refused to acknowledge. And Father . . . he was wound up in a tizzy, rarely the doting dad she saw in memories. Was she immune? Was all she'd done to find Mala, the reckless way she put herself in danger, the stubborn insistence to be involved and not give up . . .

Could it all be about Mother for me, too?

She swallowed. The question felt like an anchor on her chest. And at the moment, Usengu had to have her full attention. They had less than a day left.

"I'm going to request an audience with Father and have

Usengu formally summoned to answer for these accusations," Ariel said. "I'm also going to get the Mer–Monster Treaty amended. I'm not sure how. I'll need to think about it. Father's rigidly stubborn, but that's where I—thanks to Mother—have him outdone." She winked, and Ieka plastered on a weak grin.

"How can I help?" he asked.

"For now, stay here. I don't want to alarm Usengu. Or cause him to do anything rash. We need him to think his plan is still working. He needs to believe he's still in control. I will take a statement from you. Tell me everything you know, and we'll have it notarized so Father knows it's official. You have a Nkatafish here to certify?"

"Yes, yes, of course."

Good. The Nkatafish would rub their oily skin on the scroll's seal to secure it. Nkatas were ornery fish and only did things just so. Their oil was their pride, and they wouldn't certify authorship unless it was true. It was *known.* Ariel also needed to get word to her sisters, she realized. But could she risk anyone carrying such secret news? It might be better tell them in person. The best thing she could do was get home, and fast. "Call them and let's get the letter done. I need to get back as soon as possible."

The Nkata showed after a short wait, then finished their certifying work after a slightly longer wait. Ariel was relieved to have Ieka's words all written down and certified as authentic. She blew out a breath and tucked the sealed scroll under her arm. *This will work.*

"I *will* bring Mala back to us, Ieka. You have my word." She looked for understanding in his eyes, hoping her promise was at least some relief to him. After all, he'd been through so much—was still going through so much. But all she found was worry creased in his expression.

"Please find her, Princess."

She squeezed his fin once more, gulped down her fear, and dipped below the waterfall to rush home just as the morning sun rose on Coral Moon Festival Day.

Chapter 18

The Coral Moon, Morning

Coral Moon morning usually found the king's castle decked out in colorful garlands while horns played from the reef gardens to announce the day's beginning. Festival-themed treats and decor normally lined the halls. But that morning, the only things filling the castle were the bustling guards patrolling the corridors. There were no horns. No hint of glee. Mala's absence hung over the kingdom like a storm at the surface.

Ariel got a few funny looks as she pushed through the halls with vehement determination. But she didn't care. Her father would listen to her today. Whatever it took.

"Where is the king?" she asked a guard she passed.

"He's with his guard assembly. Princess, you're awake quite early. You shouldn't be out of your room. You—"

"Thank you." She swam past him before he could finish, down the passageway to her father's private meeting quarters. The doors were shut, but she pushed them open without hesitation. The room was jam-packed with more guards.

"Ariel?" Sebastian glanced at her in confusion, but she looked right past him. Maps were strewn across her father's desk haphazardly, and a cloud of chatter hovered over the room. Her father rubbed his chin, sullen on his throne. When he caught sight of Ariel, everything that was hard in his expression deepened.

"Ariel, what are you doing here?" He rose.

"Father." She took a deep breath and shoved out the words in a firm tone. "I need a private word with you."

"Sire?" The guard from earlier swam to Ariel's side. "Would you like me to take her back to her room?"

"You will do no such thing. I'm not a child." Eyebrows rose; her stomach burned with nerves. But she forced out the words. There was no more time to waste. She wouldn't be silenced, talked over, or ignored. Not this time. "I'm as good as Protector of my very own territory and the *only* person in this room who actually spent the last few days finding *useful* information about Mala's whereabouts! If anyone should be escorted to their room, it should be all of *you*!"

No one moved.

Her father cleared his throat. "If you'll give us the room, please. I need a word with my daughter."

They filtered out, and once the door closed behind the last guard, Ariel braced for her father's temper with her own iron determination.

"Ariel!"

"Usengu has Mala." Straight to the point. He hardly listened as it was, so she got right down to it.

"What do you mean, *Usengu*?" The shock of her words dug lines into his expression. He gripped the edge of his throne. "Usengu, my lead diplomat?" His words rang with disbelief.

"The only Usengu either of us knows, Father. I have it on good authority. I have proof."

"Proof? Where?" He held out his hand.

Ariel dug into her bag and handed over the scroll sealed by the Nkata and the stack of kelp Ieka had given her, and she explained that it wasn't Carinaean. She wasn't going to tell Father about the marriage. She couldn't. That wasn't her news to share. But she would tell him about Usengu's attack on Ieka. Her chin rose. Father *would* believe her.

He scanned the kelp and tossed it on his table. "What am I supposed to make of scribbled messages on kelp?"

"Father, Usengu tricked Ieka into leaving that note we found near the memorial! You can see his finprints on the kelp!" How could he not understand? Ariel realized she had a fist full of her woven bag. He had to believe her.

The king's mouth parted, ruminating on all she was saying. "No." He sat back. "This can't be. Usengu has known each of you since you were children. When I brought him to court, it took forever to even convince him to take the role as Overseer, and it was even harder to get him to take the honored distinction of being my right hand. That serpent doesn't have a selfish vertebra in his thorax."

"I've been to Chaine. Ieka was bound, tied up!" Ariel insisted. "And it all makes sense with what Silius and Tolum said."

King Triton shook his head harder. "I have the greatest minds in this ocean around this table overturning every stray piece of kelp in the entire sea to find your sister!" His voice thundered. "And you're expecting me to believe it's my right-hand advisor that is responsible?"

Ariel refused to back down. "I am, and you *must* call the Delegate Council to meet. Bring him here without letting him know there's any suspicion, and once he's here, make him answer for his crime! Test his finprints against the ones on the kelp!"

"Your musings have spun out of control." He paced now, ignoring her. "I know you're just trying to help, but you've gone too far."

"Father!" Anger roiled through her. She fumed.

"We have hardly a *day* left to find your sister and you're interrupting with *this*? Speculation on the word of *Ieka*, no less? I never wanted Ieka in that position in the first place. I put him in to keep a closer eye on him."

His words pinched an ache in her heart she'd thought was well buried. He wasn't going to listen. "Your narrow mind . . ." Her voice broke; the words stuck in her throat. She'd given this all she could, and her father was a wall of obstinacy in her way.

"Excuse me?" His brows pinched.

She didn't care to spare his feelings anymore. He had to know how foolish he was being. "Your narrow mind . . . is going to get my sister killed," she said, summoning her last bit of fight.

He stared at her, aghast, like he was seeing her truly for the first time.

"Your mother would turn in her grave if she could see your flagrant disregard for your own life. Guards!" His yell boomed so loud it unsteadied Ariel. The doors burst open. "I want *ten* of you to take my daughter in hand and escort her to her room! *Ten!* You will stand watch outside of her door and window," he ordered, and his guards' countenances fell. "And if she so much as moves a fin's distance away from her room, I want to know about it!"

"Yes, Sire." One of the swordfish grabbed Ariel, and her body stiffened in his clutches. They surrounded her, pulling her out of the door. She couldn't have resisted if she tried.

"I'll never forgive you for this," she muttered as her father's door shut in her face.

The walls in Ariel's room felt like they were closing in. She tossed her FastFins against the wall. She hadn't even had a chance to return them to storage before she'd been locked in her room. Father was impossible. She could hear the guards speaking to Sebastian outside of her door. She glanced at her window and saw guards pacing out there, too.

Ariel threw herself onto her bed, rubbing her wrists together as wails pulled at her throat, some mangled mess of fury and sorrow burning through her. Father was so stubborn, and her sister would pay for it with her life.

She ached from the inside out as images of the memorials that would be erected for her sister beside her mother sank her into despair. Pulled at her like a haunting spirit she couldn't shake.

Things would have been so different if Mother had been there. Everything would be different. She shook her head as Mother's face slithered through her memory like a summoned ghost. The weight of it was too much. She had to get up. To move, to do something before the weight ripped her in two.

"I can't do this. I can't—" She'd worked herself up into a mess. She slumped down on the ground and pulled her seagrass blanket, the one that Mother had made for her, from the bed and wrapped it around herself. She closed her eyes and imagined it was a hug. Pictured its strands as skin against hers, warm and comforting.

"I can't do it without you, Mom." The words broke free from her lips before she could guard herself against them. "I don't know how I have this long." She couldn't quiet the woe, the pain. Her heart was wrenching from its very depths; she couldn't control it. "But I can't do any more of it without you. I—I thought finding Mala would make missing you hurt less. Somehow. But I can't bear the weight of it. I miss you both, and nothing I can do will fix it. Nothing!"

Sitting took too much effort, so she lay, curled up, her tail twirled around her. Tight, tight, the way she imagined it felt when Mother would hold her.

"Mother is gone," she muttered with a finality she had to choke down, rubbing her wrists together. Hearing herself say it out loud somehow felt more real. She lifted herself up on her elbows. "I can't bring her back. . . ."

The painful truth of it loosed something in her. She'd been so sure her family hadn't faced their grief, but had she?

I haven't.

The truth broke her. And somehow soothed her all the same.

Ariel pulled herself up off the ground and faced herself in the looking glass. How had she been so blind? Her mother's death sat on her chest, too, heavy and cumbersome. Sea debris that strangled her no matter how she situated it. She toyed with the pieces of her that looked like Mother; her hair, the curve of her lips. She stroked the pebble on her wrist. She couldn't summon her mother's face, but she could still remember her songs. She hummed and imagined it was her Mother's voice.

"Mother always sang," she told herself, allowing herself to open the box of memories she'd refused to touch. Somehow not opening it had turned into pretending it wasn't there. "She sang all the time." She still couldn't picture her face, but she could almost smell her when she closed her eyes. "It was always the same songs." She hummed louder, rubbing her wrists harder, but despite her sorrow, she smiled.

Mother was gone.

She closed her eyes and slid one more imaginary box to the forefront of her thoughts, one her hands trembled at the thought of opening. But she knew now she had to face it fully, or she'd be in a worse prison than just her room. *Say the words, Ariel.*

"Mother is gone." Those came easier this time. "And . . ." She gripped her desk. "And it's not my fault." And neither was Mala's kidnapping. She wasn't to blame, even though it felt like she carried it square on her shoulders. That didn't mean looking for her sister was wrong. She knew she was right, but she couldn't continue using it as a veil to keep from acknowledging how much she missed Mother.

Ariel tugged at the stone on her bracelet and rolled it around in her fingers, imagining the day Father had strung it around her wrist. So many merfolk said how similar she was to Mother. She opened her eyes and stared back at the girl in the mirror, pulling her locs out of her face and pushing her shoulders back with newfound determination. Her mother had given Ariel her determined spirit, her love of other's differentness, her daring to explore the unknown. Though she could hardly remember her, she *was* like her mother, she realized. And perhaps she could find comfort in her loss by honoring her. By being true to her wanderer's heart. By trusting herself.

Somehow, she would save Mala.

But not in avoidance of grieving Mother. In honor of her.

A knock at the door pulled her from her thoughts. What could the guards possibly want? She was already being held captive.

"Yes?"

"Open up." The familiar voice was high-pitched.

"Huh?" *Either the guard on duty has a really bad cold, or that was—* She whipped the door open. "Indira? Caspia?" She gasped at the line of guards who'd shrunk to the size of Ariel's thumb, flailing, yelling something in tiny voices to match their new tiny bodies. "How—"

"Shhhh!" They scooped them all up, rushed inside her room, and shut the door.

"How did you—"

Caspia winked, dropping the guards into a jar on Ariel's shelf. The tiny swordfish waved their pointed noses to and fro, flailing, but all she could hear were little squeaks.

"Oh, my gosh, you shrank them with your Song?" Ariel blinked and blinked again to be sure she wasn't dreaming. This was Caspia talking—Miss Rule Follower. "I don't understand. What are you two doing?"

"We're here to break you out!"

Chapter 19

The Coral Moon, Morning

C aspia spoke first. "We'd heard some ruckus and came looking to see what it was and saw you rush in to talk to Father in a huff. I left, but—"

"*I* started listening." Indira pushed in front of her. "And when I heard you mention the seal and the kelp from Ieka, and he *still* wouldn't listen, I called Caspia back. *We* believe you!"

It was Ariel who couldn't believe *her* ears. "Wait, you— you do?" Ariel's head was a cloud. She couldn't be hearing them right.

"Listen, Little Fry," Caspia went on. Their nickname for her was her absolute *least* favorite, but if they were really there to help, they could call her whatever they wanted.

"I know we give you a hard time," Indira said, "but we've never seen anyone stand up to Father that way."

"So we figured you must be serious," Caspia added.

"And when we really started *listening* to what you're saying . . . My goodness, Fry, if you're right and Father does nothing, Mala is going to be *killed!*" Indira shuddered.

Caspia nodded in agreement. "That's not a chance we're going to take. I mean, she's annoying as all get out, but she's our sister."

Ariel threw her arms around her sisters. "Oh, my goodness!" She squeezed them tight, and in some odd twist of kindness they hugged her back. It was more than she had hoped for. It was more than anything she could have dreamed.

"But you have to tell us. How did you find out that Ieka knew so much about what happened to Mala?" Caspia asked.

Ariel bit her lip. She couldn't tell them about Mala and Ieka's relationship. Even if they had turned over a new shell, she couldn't take chances. "Mala was just really good friends with her Resident, and Ieka is not nearly as terrifying as everyone says."

Caspia and Indira stared at her in disbelief.

"You . . . like, talked to him?"

"Like . . . up close?"

Ariel resisted rolling her eyes. Her sisters were so much like Father. But hopefully less stubborn. "You have to stop with that. Listen, we don't have much time. But when this is all said and done and Mala is back home, you're gonna sit down and listen to her tell us all about how sweet Ieka is. Anyway, we need to focus on getting Usengu here without tipping him off that we know anything. I thought if Father called an emergency Delegate Council meeting, summoning his entire court, it wouldn't alarm him."

"Hmm." Indira tapped her tail, pondering. "Caspia could fake Father's summons. Get word to the Royal Herald that the king has called an emergency meeting and to immediately disseminate it to the entire kingdom."

"You can do that?" Ariel turned to Caspia, stunned for the second time that morning.

"I can totally mimic Father's boxy scrawly writing, and I *will*." Caspia flexed her fingers.

"Hmm, but will the herald think it's legit?" Ariel liked the direction this was going, but she still wasn't sure they could pull it off.

"We should take the message to the herald on one of Father's scrolls with his seal," Indira said. "He's been drowning in meetings for days, so it's not far-fetched that he'd send one of us to deliver the message."

Caspia nodded, tapping her lip. "Indira's right. This could work."

Ariel folded her arms. "But then how do we get Father's seal and scroll?"

Caspia's eyebrows bounced as if an idea had just struck her. "I know just the thing! Leave Father and the message to the herald to me."

Ariel couldn't help a grin. "You know, for two non-rule breakers, you sure warmed up quickly."

They both shared a bashful look, though Ariel meant it as a compliment. "But this is great. It might be wild enough to work." She gnawed at her lip. They'd need a plan once Usengu got there. He was known for his silver tongue. How would they be able to convince everyone he was guilty without him spinning the story? If her father wouldn't believe her on her own, maybe he would believe all of them.

"Indira, can you use your FastFins to get to Tolum, Silius, and Tamika, update them on everything, and ask them to come here to share what they know?"

Indira's mouth dropped. "Tamika?! You want to involve Tamika?"

Ariel waved away her sister's surprise "Yes, I've been to her palace. She's on board to help."

Indira and Caspia glanced at each other in disbelief. "Is there nothing you can't do, Little Fry?" Indira hooked her arm around Ariel's neck in a tight hug and dug her knuckle into her head. Ariel shuffled away. She hated when they did that. Well, sort of. It was nice to finally not be fighting, she supposed.

"I didn't miss anything, did I?" A small voice came from behind them.

"Flounder! How'd you get in here?" Ariel asked.

Flounder swam into the room. "I was on my way to the kitchens, and, well, there's a tiny little swordfish outside your room, shaking his fins, shouting. Did you know that?"

Caspia snorted, laughing. Indira squealed.

"Thanks to these two, yes."

Flounder held out his fin, and there was one of the guards they'd apparently missed when they picked up the others. Ariel scooped him up and added him to the jar before catching Flounder up on her sisters' being down to help.

"Okay, so we have our plan," Ariel said. "Caspia is going to get the forged message to the herald without Father knowing, and Indira, you'll notify the others?"

They nodded. This was actually happening. They were going to save Mala. Ariel gazed out the window at the sky, bright with the glow of full sun.

"We have *hours* to pull this off. MerHunters are coming by dusk."

"Wait, what should the note to the herald say?" Caspia asked.

"Something like, *Upon order of the king, an emergency council meeting is called to commence this day just before dusk. All members of the court are required to attend.*"

Caspia nodded. They rehashed the plan once more before departing, and Ariel paced in her room, hoping the effect of the magic on Father's miniature guards wouldn't wear off soon.

"I can hardly be still," Flounder said, fidgeting. "You think this'll work?"

"It'll either work, or I'll be grounded for the rest of my life."

"You can do this. You can do anything!" Flounder said.

"*Hey*, I'm proud of you, too."

He smiled.

"We have to get this right, Flounder. No mistakes." She glanced at the window. Had she thought of everyone? She stewed on that question all morning until her door slid open. It was Julia with her breakfast.

"Oh, I'm sorry to interrupt, dear." She smiled. "Might I come in and tidy up a bit?"

She had an idea! Ariel tapped Julia. Her housekeeper had been with them in High Sun. Had she seen *anything* the morning Mala was kidnapped? Usengu was guilty, but the more evidence she could stack against him the better.

"I need to talk to you, please."

Julia slinked inside. "Whatever is wrong?" She clasped her jackknife claws. She looked nervous. "Was there something I missed cleaning?"

"No, nothing like that. I need to talk to you about Princess Mala."

Julia's translucent body stiffened into a hard line. "Oh, Princess, I've already told everything I know to the guards." She turned and started cleaning.

"Please, Julia, I just need to know if you saw anything unusual with . . . Usengu, the king's right hand, specifically."

Julia froze. Ariel swam around her to make her meet her eyes.

"You won't be in trouble if it's something you didn't mention to the guards, I promise."

Julia's eyes drew together in sadness. "Please—" Her voice broke. She shook her head and backed away.

Suspicion coiled in Ariel. "Julia, what do you know? Tell me, *please*."

"I never saw anything, I swear. I just . . . I just *heard* him. I was in the princess's closet, sorting her things, when someone with a deep voice came in asking Mala to come with them. I recognized the voice but couldn't place it. And Princess Mala was confused at first. So I listened harder and realized it was Usengu. I was unsure what was about to happen. Unsure what he'd do if he caught me snooping. He is not the kind helper the king thinks he is. He is *frightening* to those beneath him. I've seen the way he interrogates the Residents, the way he scolds anyone who tries to get in his business. I froze. By the time I came out, they were both gone." Julia sank onto Ariel's stool. "When the news came that she had been kidnapped and I returned to her room in shambles, I convinced myself I must have been wrong. That it wasn't Usengu. Because the room didn't look that way when I left. I was confused. A-and I was so scared to give the *wrong* information that I didn't say anything about it when the guards questioned me. What if—what if I had, and it helped? I didn't want to be seen as responsible. I didn't know what to do, so I told myself I'd never say a word. It wouldn't bring her back."

Her head drooped with regret, and Ariel cradled the loyal housekeeper. Usengu could have lured Mala out like Ursula had lured her mother, and then returned to make her room look as though a stranger, someone Mala feared, had broken in. He'd broken the Safety Seal to frame a Resident, so returning to the room wasn't that far-fetched. There were many reasons the room might have looked that way. Usengu was clever, especially with words. Look what he'd done with the kelp to send them on a wild hunt of misinformation. But regardless, Mala's kidnapping wasn't Julia's fault. Even had she said something, would Father have listened?

"Oh, Julia. You've probably been so torn up about this. There's nothing you could have done. I would have never guessed that the enemy was within our own walls."

"You believe me?" Her brows drew together.

She hugged her tighter. "Julia, you've been like a mother to me and my sisters since Mother died. Of course I believe you. Usengu does have Mala. You were right."

She gasped. "And you're sure?"

"I am."

"He is as good as a brother to your father." She shook her head fretfully. "That will not be news the king will receive well."

"I know. Julia, I need you to do a huge favor for me."

She shook her head, already inferring what Ariel likely wanted. "Oh, child, what would he say? What would he think of me keeping this secret all this time as they investigated?"

"This isn't your fault. Please, talk to Father with me." It was her last-ditch effort to convince him. He'd never question Julia's honor. Even if she hadn't said anything then, there was no way Mala's kidnapping was her fault. "For Mala, please?"

Julia took a deep breath before nodding. "For Mala."

Chapter 20

The Coral Moon, Afternoon

The morning had passed by the time her father answered Ariel's request for an audience, though she'd stressed that it was a very serious emergency. Flounder was off being scarce. She'd told him to keep a stealthy eye on things. Truly, she didn't want him being blamed if this thing fell apart. She double-checked that the containers with the mini guards were well hidden behind her bed. Ariel paced, arranging and rearranging the things on her desk. This had to work. The herald had gotten the messages off all right, so the council would be arriving soon, and Father would have no idea he'd called an assembly. She had to get to him and convince him to play along. But first he had to believe her.

Knock. Knock.

"Come—" But the door swung open before she could answer. Father's hair was unkempt, and tired lines hugged his eyes. His whole face seemed to have thinned in just a matter of hours; his cheeks were sunken. He hadn't slept in who knew how long. This was wearing on him.

"Julia, good day." He dipped his chin in the maid's direction. "Ariel?"

"Father—"

"Your guards?" His lips thinned. "Where are they?"

She shrugged, her cheeks warming.

He sighed as if he didn't have energy to even be angry. "Well? I have much on my plate right now, as you can imagine. What is it you needed? I was told it was an emergency."

"I need you to listen, Father," Ariel said.

Triton narrowed his eyes, waving her away as he turned around to head back out of the door. "Ariel, I already told you that I don't have time—"

"To me," Julia cut in, and the king snapped his mouth shut, curiosity deepening the exhaustion carved into his brow.

"What could you possibly have to say, Julia, that is so pressing in this moment?"

Ariel listened as Julia recalled everything. Father opened his mouth to interrupt more than once, but no words ever came out. Julia's story could hardly be questioned. He stared at Ariel with irritation, but the longer Julia talked, the more even that melted away. When she finished, her father's shoulders hung heavy with a familiar weight. Grief was a fishing line around his throat.

"And you're sure it was Usengu you heard?"

"Yes, Sire. I tried to convince myself I wasn't at the time out of fear, but I've thought on it again and again since that day, and I can't deny it was him. I—I just assumed maybe I didn't have the whole story, or someone came in after him, or there was an explanation or something."

"So you're saying . . ." But he couldn't finish. He buried his face in his hands and turned his back on the both of them. She had him. He was listening, it seemed, truly listening, and he believed them.

"Father, forgive me. This was the only way I could make you see."

His head hung from his sinking shoulders, and he sat on Ariel's jelly stool. His lips parted several times and closed before any words actually came out. "No, it is I who needs to beg for your forgiveness. I'm hardly worthy of it." His lips pressed together.

Julia's brows kissed in regret. "I am so sorry, Sire." Her voice cracked, and Ariel set a hand on her.

"Julia," the king said, rubbing his fists together, "your

love for this family and my girls could never be questioned. Thank you for telling me." He sighed and shook his head. "Please, take the next several days to do something just for you, something you like."

"That is very gracious, My King." She beamed. Ariel thanked her housekeeper and bid her goodbye. It was just she and Father, and Ariel's stomach twisted with worry. He believed her. She'd defied him a hundred times, but surely he had to see why?

"It's like reliving the tragedy of your mother all over again." He shook his head. "I miss them both so much, you know, Ariel. I couldn't—" He exhaled, but it stuck in his chest as he rubbed his wrists together without hiding it. This time he didn't turn to shield his face. "With your mother, that's on my shoulders. I should have kept a firmer hand on things. My father told me how treacherous these waters are, and I . . . Your mother loved adventure. She wanted to visit every territory in the ocean if she could." He stilled for several moments, trying to find the words.

Ariel was frozen, silent. She'd never heard her father open up so much.

"I thought if I'd just been firmer, kept more control over things, she'd be . . . she'd be here," he said. He looked down, unable to meet Ariel's eyes. "This is my fault, can't you see that? I did this."

"No, Father." Ariel said. She swam over to him, cupping his cheek and coaxing him to look at her. She was sure about one thing. "Mother's death is no one's fault but Ursula's."

Her father looked at her.

"Tamika told me. And Mala—*who we are going to save—* being kidnapped is no one's fault but Usengu's. Torturing ourselves with blame only imprisons us in our grief."

Her father raked his fingers through his gray hair. Up close, Ariel could see in his heavy eyelids just how stressed he was. She remembered a time when his skin glowed. When he smiled more than he frowned. Now the curl of his lips was a permanent grimace. Father hadn't taken care of himself in a long time.

"You've not been the same since Mother died," Ariel said. It was the first time she had said the words out loud. "It's like pieces of you have been melting away over the years."

King Triton gave her a tight smile. "I'll be fine, sweet Ariel. It's you all I'm worried about. Your mother lived so boundlessly. She was so . . . trusting. See where trust has led us."

"You're wrong, Father. I've learned so much from Sea Monsters."

"You say that, but how many have you met?" the king said. "What? A handful?"

"Father, I know you find it silly. But we have much to learn from Sea Monsters and others unlike us. Your father and his before him would have you believe differently, but they were wrong. And their ideas have poisoned you. Mother dying only cemented them. But you have to crack those walls, rip them down. They will crush you. They will crush all of us." She took his hands. "Mother had some of it right. Can't you see? If it weren't for Silius and Tolum and Ieka—yes, Ieka the Notorious—we wouldn't even have the chance to save Mala."

The king didn't speak for several moments. "If you are right, and Usengu is behind this . . ."

"I am right," Ariel insisted. "But Usengu doesn't represent all Sea Monsters. You can't define an entire species by the actions of one or two. It seems each person's actions should speak for themselves. Everyone should have a chance to prove who they are before the world decides it for them." She'd tried this with him before, and he had never gotten it. But she could only hope his softened heart gave him better hearing. "You blame them all for Mother. That's what it is. You keep your circle tight and don't let anyone in. You call it love, and sure, that's part of it, but it's ultimately fear, Father. And you can't live like that. And look, look at the mess that's made. Where the Sea Monsters who've helped us, you are determined to keep at arm's length. And the one you hold close has betrayed you. This way of doing things, of shunning people and wielding trust like a weapon, doesn't work!" She considered bringing up Ursula to further illustrate how he was just wrong. But she hesitated to sear the wound too much. She wanted him to listen, not close his ears in anger.

He was silent.

Had she gone too far? Her chest heaved as she hung on the tension in the air, waiting for his retort. Had she pierced through to the meat of him? Or was there still some guard he held up she couldn't see?

Bum, bum, babum!

A hornfish blew. It was the Royal Herald; a council member had arrived.

"What's that herald going on about?" the king asked. "We cancelled the festival with everything going on with Mala. We don't have any visitors scheduled for today."

Ariel put on her best smile. "Actually, about that . . ."

"What have you done?" His tone was tight, but his eyes were still warm.

"I'll tell you, Father. But you've gotta trust me." Her brows rose in a challenge. The hornfish blared again and again, twelve times in rapid succession.

"The *entire* Delegate Council is here?" His mouth fell open. She nodded.

He rubbed his temples. "Go on, then. Explain yourself." He gave her his attention, and his usual glaring frustration wasn't there. He hadn't fully come around to her way of things, but something she'd said had cracked those hard walls inside him. It was a start. At the very least, she was relieved he actually appeared to want to know her plan.

"I know you're scared, Father. I'm scared, too. But I know what needs to be done here. We have to handle Usengu just so. He has the Sea Monsters' ears. Their hearts. That's powerful, Father."

He huffed a laugh. "Spoken like a wise diplomat."

Ariel smiled, realizing she'd impressed him. "Promise you'll trust me?" She stuck out her hand so they could shake on it.

"You have my word, Ariel." He shook her hand. "I'll follow your lead."

Chaos filled the castle. Ariel led the way out of her room, down the corridor, and into the foyer, where an army of seafolk shouted. The walls buckled with people, some yelling for answers to rumors about the king and others shuffling along amid the ruckus. Several Ariel recognized as council members, and others she didn't. It appeared more than the Delegate Council had heard about the summons. She spotted Flounder hanging back in the shadows, keeping a distance, but keeping an eye on things.

"End Triton's reign," a group of seafolk chanted. "The king cannot be trusted!"

Ariel froze. Silius and Tolum had warned her, but she hadn't yet seen it for herself. The crowd was irate. Ariel recognized some of the same faces from her Protector Ceremony, such as the fish who'd stormed out when Father didn't answer his question.

"I never thought I'd see the day," her father breathed. The shouts blared in Ariel's ears.

Her nails dug into her palm. Somehow she had to keep control of things. Usengu was the true enemy. Father had work to do, too, and she fully intended to hold him to it. But first she had to save Mala.

"Usengu has turned them against us with rumors," Ariel said, remembering what Ieka had told her. Some of them were true, but she wasn't going to add fuel to the fire.

Her father shoved through the crowd, gesturing for his guards. "Order in my court or, so help me, I'll have all of you dragged out of here!" Father's voice boomed over the crowd in that commanding way it had, but hardly made a dent. The shouting roared over him.

"Guards?" Ariel called, but Father's guards didn't respond. *"Guards!"*

"Do you hear the princess?" her father asked them. "Listen to her, and do precisely what she says."

The guards' lips tightened, but their eyes shifted to her with nods.

"Thank you." Ariel squeezed her father's arm in thanks. "We're going to get Mala back."

Her father smiled at her, and she warmed all over.

"Guards," she went on. "If you would, please get this assembly into the Grand Room and assure them their concerns will be heard. Say whatever you need to pacify them. And for the love of anything good—be nice!"

The guards hesitated before bowing and swimming off.

"Excuse me, pardon me." She squeezed through a shoving match between a mollusk and an eel. Ariel pushed through the raucous crowd, looking for some glimpse of Usengu.

"Out of my way, you half human," someone said, but whether it was to her or someone else, she couldn't tell. She swam faster, looking for some sign of her sisters, Silius, or Tolum. The crowd wasn't just angry at Father; they were fighting among themselves. Chaos could be contagious like that. Ariel caught a glimpse of light purple hair.

"Karina!" She waved and exhaled.

"Lula!" Karina barreled into her with a hug, and Perla was close behind her.

"You came?" She hadn't expected them.

"Of course we came. We heard the council summons and didn't want to miss anything."

Ariel pulled them aside and updated them in her best whisper on everything they'd learned, including the conversation with Father and Julia. Their eyes swelled. But she put a finger to their lips. "No one knows yet, just the family. Help me get everyone into the Grand Room, please. If you see *him*, you know who I mean . . . act normal."

"Understood." Karina nodded.

Her sisters swam off. And Ariel watched as, bit by bit, guards ushered the angry council delegates through the foyer and into the Grand Room, assuring them they'd been called in for good reason and their concerns would be heard. She was turning to find Father again when a cold, slimy fin curled around her shoulder.

"Oh, dear Princess." It was Usengu, his eyes thinned suspiciously. "Are you all right?"

She sanitized her expression before facing him. "Y-yes, Usengu. You're so kind to ask."

"Don't worry, I'll calm this crowd. Who knows what they're going on about this time?" He cleared his throat. "But that's my job, isn't it? Keeping things in line." He stroked her face, and bile rose in Ariel's throat. "I'm curious why the king has called such a last-minute assembly."

"Princess Mala is still missing." She kept her face stoic, void of knowing. "So I assume he has an update for us. What else could it be about?" She couldn't resist. She had to see his reaction.

"Oh, *yes*." He barely flinched, but Ariel caught it. "You're right. That makes sense. I should check in with him and see if there's anything I missed in my travels today. I certainly hope it's a good update." His mouth pushed sideways as if he was trying to read her. "We could use some good news around here, especially with what happened to your mother so many years ago. Don't you think?"

"Yes." She met his eyes, fury hanging on her tongue. How dare he speak of her mother? How dare he pretend . . . so, so well! Her nostrils flared, her chest heaving with rage. A crowd swam between them, and Usengu held her stare without a blink. There was a challenge in his eyes, in the set of his jaw. Had he always been this transparent? Or was she just better at seeing him? Could he know she knew? Fear fluttered through her. What would he do if he knew they were on to him?

She pulled from her very depths the gentlest tone she could muster. "I am just so grateful"—she grabbed his fins and gave them a squeeze—"that we have your support."

"Of course." His lips split in a smile, and he bowed. "I live to serve your father and this family, Princess. It is my greatest ambition."

Ugh. She could have retched. "Well, I should be going." She swallowed the bile rising in her throat.

"Of course." Usengu watched as she swam off, and she could still feel his slimy touch all over her. She spotted Indira and Caspia talking to someone with brown hair. *Is that—*

"Tamika?"

As she joined their huddle, Indira and Caspia threw their arms around Tamika. Ariel wasn't sure what she'd missed, but this was certainly the highlight of it.

"You're here!"

"Because of you, Riri. Thank you for bringing me back home." Tamika set a glowing shell in Ariel's hands. "This is from Silius. Indira let him know your request, but the cost was too great. He hopes you can understand."

His ancestors' memories. He'd lose them all.

"Of course I do. Thank you." She studied the purple glow inside the shell. "What is it?"

"A memory." She closed her hand around her sister's. "I hope it helps."

"Thank you, Tamika. And hopefully Tolum can address the rumors that have been spread." She gazed around, hoping for some sight of him. None yet.

"Wait until Father sees this," Perla said, butting in.

Ariel smiled. That was the silver lining in it all. She tightened her grip on the memory from Silius. It wasn't the same as his being there, but it was something. "You all should get inside for assembly," she said. "Time isn't on our side."

"It's true, then? We have until dusk, when the sky turns pink?" Tamika said.

The words stuck in Ariel's throat, so she nodded instead.

"That's no time at all. We should be going to wherever Usen—"

Ariel pressed a finger to Tamika's lips. "He doesn't know we know," she whispered. "Go on, inside."

They swam inside, and Ariel looked yet again for some sign of Tolum. But there was none. The last bit of the crowd filtered into the Grand Room, and Ariel noted the sun starting its descent, flickering through a window. The world swayed. Tamika was right to panic. The moon would be coral pink very soon. They needed to prove Usengu was the true culprit behind these schemes, and *fast*.

Chapter 21

The Coral Moon, Afternoon

She could have cut the tension in the Grand Room with a shard of obsidian. Ariel clutched the statement from Ieka, certified by the Nkatafish in Chaine, firmly in one hand and the memory from Silius in the other. *Will it be enough?*

Her father and sisters perched along the dais in a long line. Usengu sat among the council on a raised platform. The seafolk at his back watched the meeting in silence, scowls written into their disgruntled expressions. Ariel's insides quaked. Turning this crowd wasn't going to be easy. They seemed to want Father off the throne. Did that mean they wanted Usengu *on* it? *What is his motive, exactly?* Sebastian hung near Father's throne, whispering in his ear.

"What's the meaning of this meeting?" a blue octopus called out from the gallery.

"Quiet down, please," Sebastian said. "I turn it over to you, Sire."

King Triton clenched his fist. He glared at Usengu.

"Father," Ariel whispered. "Please, let me speak."

"And I hand it over," he said, shoving the words between his teeth, "to Princess Ariel. She has a word for all of you."

Eyes darted around the room in surprise at the king's giving someone else the stage.

Ariel smoothed her trembling hands over her tail. She hadn't imagined standing up there in front of everyone to call Usengu out by herself. The sky shone through the glass dome overhead, deepening its golden hue. It was now or never.

"I—"

The doors cracked open and in swam Tolum, his whale body wiggling to get through the tight entryway.

"Tolum!" Ariel yelled with glee.

"What is the meaning of this?" Usengu rose from his seat. "A Resident outside of his territory, unless specifically summoned by the king or his right hand, is unheard of," he barked. "And entirely improper. Sire, do you want me to—"

"Usengu, sit down," Ariel said sharply. Usengu's mouth

parted, his eyes drawn up as if her sharp tone wounded him. He looked to the king.

"You heard the princess," her father said. "Sit. Tolum, good to see you again."

"Tolum, thank you for coming," Ariel added.

"Of course, My King, Princess," Tolum said.

From his spot with the council, Usengu met her eyes, but because she knew him, had known him for so long, the usual warmth she felt had dissolved and all that was behind his eyes was a hard glare.

Ariel gulped down her last bit of nerves and faced the gallery. "Seafolk of the court, we've summoned you here today to bear witness to a great travesty." She hesitated. What would happen when she revealed the truth? Could this really work?

Her father sat, teeth dug into his knuckle. Indira and Caspia held hands. Perla winked at her, and Karina nodded for her to go on. Ariel swallowed hard, and her eyes found Tamika. Her long-lost sister smiled, holding a palm to her chest. She could feel her family's comfort from across the room, and it gave her the strength to continue.

"You are all aware my sister, Princess Mala, was taken a few days ago," Ariel said. She set her jaw and pointed at Usengu. "*He* kidnapped my sister. He knows where she is being kept, and he intends to hand her over to MerHunters this evening, at dusk . . . just like Ursula did to the queen."

Gasps exploded in the chamber, then quickly turned to shouts. Those Usengu had turned to his side glared, but she couldn't tell if it was in surprise or in disbelief.

"And I have proof," Ariel shouted over them, and to her surprise, they quieted.

"What is this?" Usengu shot up and approached the dais, seething with anger. Whether he felt resentment over being caught or actual remorse, Ariel wasn't sure, nor did she care.

Father pointed the trident at him. Gold sparked from its sharp tips and surrounded Usengu, holding him in place. "Go on, Ariel."

Usengu writhed but couldn't break free.

"As you know, Tolum is Resident in the Saithe Sea. Tolum, could you please come forward?" Ariel gestured to the Resident, who shyly swam forward, anxiously looking at the crowd. "Sebastian, can you let the gallery know the gift the king bestowed on Tolum when he was sworn in as Resident?"

"That would be, uhh . . ." Sebastian pressed his monocle to his eye and skimmed his notes. *"Veriselim.* The inability to lie. Whatever he tells us, we can count on as true."

"Thank you, Sebastian. Tolum, can you please share what you know with the council?"

The Resident hesitated, avoiding Usengu's glare, and

then recounted the rumors he'd heard about tensions being high between Sea Monsters and mermaids. The source of those rumors, he'd been told, was someone trustworthy from the castle, but he never wanted to assume who it was. He'd heard that Father was gathering up Sea Monsters and locking them away. That he was starting with Carinae. That the Mer–Monster Treaty was going to be amended so that only royal merfolk had the freedom to move about the seas, and restrictions were going to get even tighter. "And every creature I asked said the same thing—they'd heard it from someone trustworthy from the castle. So they'd taken them at their word."

"And who do you think your community would deem trustworthy from the castle? Or have communication with from the castle?"

"I mean, I guess I hadn't even thought about that. The king hasn't been our way in ages. The only contact they'd have with anyone from the court is with Usengu."

Exactly. He was the only one from the castle who frequented the territories beside Resident and Protector. If someone from the castle was stirring up lies, it could only be him. And from him, they would of course be believable.

"One more question, Tolum," Ariel said. "What motive do you think Usengu might have for doing something like this?"

The Sea Monster tapped his lip. "Well, it seems to me like he just wanted to get everyone upset to make his own play for the royal throne. Why else turn people against their king?"

Brows cinched, eyes darting between Ariel and Usengu and the king. The glares that had burned at her moments earlier began to shift in uncertainty. It was the in she needed.

And I thank you for it, Tolum. "Sowing discord, spreading gossip. And now this from Silius in Fracus."

Heads swiveled in every direction, expecting Silius to join them. Ariel held up the translucent shell from the Fracus Resident, its purple light throbbing.

"A memory," someone uttered.

"Sebastian? Can you confirm Silius's gift?"

"Um . . ." He squinted at his notes. "Dear goodness, my handwriting is frightful. Okay, here it is. Silius, Resident in Fracus Sea. That would be Princess Tamika's territory. He—"

"Silius possesses all the memories of all his kind." Tamika rose, and every eye in the place snapped to her. "He can share them at will as well—store them in shells, as you see here. Though if he ever leaves his territory, he'll lose them. He's extracted this, and my own Nkatafish certified its authenticity."

Sebastian inspected the shell, his reading monocle pressed to his face. "It's indeed sealed and secure."

Ariel cracked open the shell, and the purple light throbbed brighter until the whole room glowed with its radiance. She watched as the light beamed and every pupil in the room glowed purple. Everything went black. Ariel blinked and saw a hazy memory unfolding before her. It was Silius, and he was untying a fish from a weird circular contraption lodged around its neck.

"Thank you, sir," the frogfish said. "Was afraid I'd end up merfood."

"Don't be silly," Silius said.

"Oh, I wasn't joking. Or haven't you heard?"

Silius's forehead creased in confusion.

"I heard the king's changing all the rules. Nothing's gonna be like it was, see. Fish like me, little guys, we'll be the king's daughters' appetizers."

"Princess Tamika would never—"

"How do you know? She never comes out of that fortress. Mark my word. I have it on good authority, someone from the castle themselves said the king's daughters are coming for all of us, starting with Chaine. Something is going down there. The Protector there is forcing Ieka—"

"Ieka the Notorious?"

"Yeah, the big scary guy, forcing him to do something really bad. My buddy didn't have the details. Just told us to steer clear. You won't catch me near the palace. You and Usengu rule these waters, far as I'm concerned." He tipped his head. "I best be getting along. Watch your back, sir."

The world faded to purple. Ariel blinked, and the room came back into focus. Every eye in the room was batting, the effects of the memory wearing off. They'd all seen it. Silius's encounter with the fish left no room for argument.

"You've seen it all for yourselves!"

Ariel turned to a sea otter in the audience whose expression had gone from rage to confusion. "Kind sir, there in the audience, have you heard any of these rumors mentioned today as well?"

He swallowed. "I have."

"And who told them to you?"

He swallowed, and his eyes snapped to a tight-lipped Usengu. "The Overseer of Residents and right hand of the king, Usengu."

The crowd mumbled and nodded in agreement over the rumors they, too, had heard. Usengu's eyes bulged as he wriggled harder against the king's magic.

And there it is. The truth.

"He's spread lies all over the kingdom to hide his dirty work." She pulled out the testimony from Ieka and held it up for the wide-eyed crowd, now silent with suspicion. "And here's a note from Ieka—yes, Ieka the Notorious—telling you plainly how Usengu bound him up and used him."

Sebastian looked it over. "This is also certified authentic."

"As you know," Ariel went on, "Ieka in Chaine works closely with Princess Mala."

"Real close, I heard," someone shouted.

"Too close," another said.

"*And!*" She raised her voice over theirs. She wouldn't be thrown off track. Nor would she have her sister's secret shared behind her back. She told them everything her investigation had yielded, how Ieka had been forced to write a fraudulent message to mislead their search. Her sisters stared in awe as she laid out proof after proof to build a convincing case against Usengu. Father was rendered speechless as well, impressed with her. Even Sebastian's monocle had fallen off his face.

"I don't need to hear any more! Guards!" Triton pulled back his trident to release Usengu for arrest. The serpent wriggled, stretching his fins.

"Sire!" he pleaded, and the discussion in the crowd ceased. "I have served your family for years. I've been *gravely* accused. *Wrongly* accused. The law allows for a defense. Might I have an opportunity to speak?"

Her father's jaw clenched. Ariel froze. *No, no. His silver tongue cannot be trusted!* Silence hung over them as Ariel's heart thudded in her ears.

"Fath—"

"Granted," her father said, and a piece of Ariel shattered.

Usengu slithered forward and Ariel watched with dismay, hoping he didn't destroy everything she'd just proven.

"I remember when this one was a wee little fry," Usengu began, working his way around the room. "Oosen, she used to call me. 'Would you show me that trick?' she would ask. And I would do it. A little trick my own mother taught me, turning stones different colors. She would laugh, and it was the only reward I'd ever wanted. All of them were that way. You see, I lost my family at a young age and was lucky to find work in the library here. The king ran into me one day, and I impressed him with all I knew of Sea Monsters. I've done nothing but serve him faithfully since. To see such an accusation laid on my head, by the family I've so lovingly worked with . . . friends, my heart is grieved."

Usengu faced Father. "My King, I have *never* wished anything ill to you or your honorable family. I do not know this frogfish in Silius' memory. Never met him. Lies, I tell you, it's all lies. From jealousy, perhaps?" He swam closer to her father. "Beasts can be seedy, untrustworthy characters. We both know this, My King."

He turned to Tolum. "I do not know why Tolum and the others would credit me for stirring up these rumors." He held up a fin. "To be clear, I heard them, too. But that is the nature of being in a position like mine. I have the king's ear, as all of you know. So, of course, others would try to come between that."

Ariel studied her father's face, desperate to see it rigid and stern. But the lines had softened some, and she could see the questions warring in him. He and Usengu had known each other for so long. He didn't want to believe any of it was true, and Usengu knew that. He was using it. But Ariel could see through him. She needed a new plan.

"My King," Usengu went on, "there is some truth to what your dear daughter said. I do know where Mala is. In fact, when I received your summons for this assembly, I was actually on my way here anyway to bring you urgent news. You see, I'd just intercepted some intel about where Princess Mala is supposedly being kept. It is a spot in Fracus at Fisher's Kitchen. The known place where MerHunters lurk. I was just about to tell you these things, Sire, before all of these accusations began brewing."

Father glared, then glanced at Ariel.

"Mala is there, you're sure?" King Triton's jaw clenched.

"Yes. I had the men with me hold the beasts who were carrying this treasonous information. They are yours to interrogate. Sire, let me show you." He lowered his tone. "Let me take you there myself and prove that all I say is true."

Doubt rose like a noxious weed through Ariel. Was Usengu being . . . honest? Had she missed something? No, she wouldn't second-guess herself. Her instincts were right. She had to trust herself. Usengu was trying to trick Father. If he could deliver the king to these MerHunters, he could take Father's place.

She wasn't going to let that happen. She needed to bait him with something he wouldn't refuse. But what? What could she offer that was worth more than a throne?

Then it hit her.

Ariel cleared her throat. "It's hard to know what to believe, Usengu. My word is against yours. But if what you say is true, you go retrieve Mala from Fisher's Kitchen. If you bring her back here safely, Father's trident is yours."

The king's trident was the most powerful artifact in the ocean. With it, Usengu could take the throne and more.

Usengu flinched, but he looked intrigued. She'd caught him off guard. She could tell he was sifting through her words for some hint of a trick. As if the wheels in his brain were turning and had just changed directions.

"Is this true, Sire?" he asked. "You would wager such a thing?"

Ariel met her father's eyes. *You promised,* she mouthed. His stare burned with fear.

"It is as the princess says," he answered. "Bring me Mala, and in gratitude and apology for the egregious accusations laid here today, my trident is yours."

The gallery exploded in chatter.

A smile slithered across Usengu's lips. "I have one amended condition. Just to be sure there are no more accusations of foul play, Princess Ariel, you will accompany me to Fisher's Kitchen to retrieve Princess Mala."

"She will do no such thing!" her father boomed. "You will be escorted by my guards and myself."

"Actually, Sire." It was Sebastian, pressing his monocle to his face. "I've just gotten word the supply of FastFins have been damaged. It seems there is no way to get there quickly."

"I was hurrying here, Sire, so I didn't even think to take mine off." Usengu flicked his tail, and it shimmered. Ariel burned with irritation. Had he destroyed the supply but conveniently kept his for a quick getaway? She could see through him so plainly now. He couldn't be trusted to go get Mala himself. Maybe coming back for the trident was strong enough bait, but what if it wasn't? An idea struck her.

"Actually . . ." Ariel grabbed her father's wrist. "Mine are in my room. I *will* go with you, Usengu."

"*No!*" King Triton pulled her aside, where no one could hear. "There must be another way!"

"Father, there isn't, and"—she lowered her voice to a whisper—"you promised to trust me."

"*Ariel.*"

"I know what I'm doing. No one else has intact FastFins.

Mala could be killed at any moment, Father. We're running out of time, *and* options. It's not the same as Mother. I'm going there with eyes wide open. I can do this!" She cupped the bracelet on her wrist. "I just . . . feel it in my gut. I have to be the one to do this."

His lips tightened in a thin line, and his expression pinched with pain. She couldn't think of a time she'd seen her father this scared. He nodded, begrudgingly giving his blessing, but his hand gripped the railing of his dais so hard it crunched under his fist. Ariel faced the crowd.

"We have a deal, Usengu. We'll seal it with a Promise Pact so you know it cannot be broken."

Indira and Caspia startled, and their gasps quickly turned into wails.

"Ariel, what are you doing?" It was Perla.

But Tamika grabbed her. "Riri can do this. She doesn't go alone. Mother is with her, in spirit."

Father's raised hand quieted her sisters.

She hoped so. She faced the silver-tongued monster. "I'll go with you to Fisher's Kitchen to retrieve Mala."

"Very good." He smiled, his eyes flickering with ambition. A chill rippled down Ariel's spine. She hoped she'd made the right decision.

Chapter
22

The Coral Moon, Evening

F ather wound his trident, muttering the words of the
Promise Pact. The metal prongs glowed as Usengu's
eyes widened eagerly. Ariel and her sisters watched
in shock and angst. Promise Pacts were a big deal. Ariel had
never seen one before. Father was going to wager his trident
on whether Usengu kept his word.

The Grand Room glowed with Father's magic, which surrounded him a bubble of light.

"Upon the Royal Seal of my word," he said, "I vow that
this trident should yield its allegiance to Usengu"—the light

oozed across the room to surround Usengu as well—"if he returns with Princess Mala, *alive,* before the moon turns bright coral." Father's shoulders shuddered, and more lines carved his wary countenance as the Pact glowed brighter just before the light vanished completely.

The crowd watched in awe, mouths agape, daring not even to whisper. Usengu could rule their kingdom. Father had sworn he wouldn't bargain with the kidnapper, and yet here he was doing exactly that, because she'd convinced him to. She gulped.

"It is done." Her father leaned in toward Ariel's ear. "Bring her home, Ariel. Somehow, bring her home."

Ariel squeezed her father's hand once more in reassurance before she and Usengu set off. In mere minutes, the castle was no more than a dot behind them. The deal could not be broken. And if Usengu got the trident, the kingdom would likely follow shortly after.

I have to save Mala and the Seven Seas. I cannot fail.

She followed Usengu at a distance the entire way to Fisher's Kitchen. Knowing how adamant he had been about her coming along sent a shiver down her arms. There was no way she could allow Usengu to go back with Mala and collect that trident. The only way to fix this was to retrieve Mala herself and get back first, making it impossible for Usengu to meet the terms of the Pact.

Usengu will pay for his crimes.

He didn't say a word to her the entire trip. Ariel could see his beady little mind working on how he was going to pull this off. She wasn't sure what sort of deal he'd made with the MerHunters, but her discovering his dirty work had thrown him, she could tell.

She recognized the shift in landscape as they approached Fracus. The underwater craters were more vast and desolate, scant of foliage as the colorful ocean faded into earth tones. The water grew warmer the closer they got to Fisher's Kitchen.

"Just a little further, Princess."

Ariel searched his gaze, for what, she wasn't sure, but only darkness stared back at her. Usengu skirted a corner, and Ariel felt everything inside her go limp. She recognized the colossal pillars of rock he darted and dashed between. They were near the spot where Mother had died. The realization haunted her, but she kept close to Usengu's tail until he stopped suddenly.

"Wait here."

"I'm not waiting anywhere." Her words came out bolder than she felt. "Where is Mala?"

"Shhh, would you?" Usengu ducked behind a rock, ignoring her question. What was he watching out for? What was he planning?

The sky brooded above the water, burning orangey pink. The time was near. They had to hurry. She had to grab Mala and go before . . . before . . .

"Where is she?" she asked again, having no time for patience with her sister's life on the line.

"Would you shut up!" Usengu growled. "You've been a thorn in my side. How did you find out about Ieka, anyway?" Ariel's eyes widened in surprise. It was the first time Usengu had ever spoken to her so harshly. Although she had known he had been deceiving them, it was still a shock to hear the difference in his tone. Ariel stroked her purple pebble bracelet, trying to calm herself down. She wasn't sure what he was plotting, but the Coral Moon would be rising at any moment. She wouldn't be threatened or kept quiet, not now. She was too close to finding her sister!

"The Safety Seal wasn't working," Ariel said, "and there's only a short list of fish who could have fiddled with it."

"That *stupid* fish from Chaine!" Usengu cursed. "Some buddy of Ieka's waiting at the barrier to get access so he could tell on me to the king. I got rid of him, all right, but I must have screwed up the seal in the process." He scowled. "I should have been more careful," he muttered to himself, turning away from her to keep an eye on something. What, Ariel wasn't quite sure. "I should have left her room intact, o-or skipped the ransom note. Or maybe cleaned up our tracks when she broke out of that net I worked around her. Somehow you put this together, and not in the way I hoped." He smiled wryly and tapped his head. "Fortunately, I'm cleverer than you think. Now shut it, right now, I mean it!"

But Ariel refused to listen to him.

"Mala! Mala! Are you there?" she called out, ignoring Usengu's protest.

"Relle!" someone called back.

Mala's voice.

Ariel's heart sped up. Her sister was here. She was indeed *alive.* Her heart swelled. She darted in the direction of her sister's voice. She expected to see Usengu on her tail, but he wasn't behind her. She darted around in search of her sister. "Mala? Mala, keep talking. Where are you?"

"Here, Relle! I'm here!"

Ariel swam through boulders and around a steep drop-off until she found herself in shallower water. Across a bed of desert reef, she spotted her sister, bound to a rock. She rushed over and tugged at the ties wrapped around Mala. Ariel gulped down the lump in her throat. *My sister. She's alive!* Her heart leapt as she worked furiously at her ties.

"You're okay, I'm here!"

"You came. You really came," Mala said, her face pinched with fear. "I was worried you'd never find me in the desolate cave he kept me in. Then today he brought me up here, and I—I was so sure—" Her voice broke.

"I'm going to save you."

"But how did you—"

"We figured out it was Usengu, thanks to Ieka."

Their eyes met.

"I'm so happy for you, Mala, really."

Mala bit her lip, and Ariel could feel the weight of her joy and relief at what she'd just said. At knowing her secret wasn't just hers anymore. Ariel tugged and pulled. By the time she undid the last tie that held Mala in place, she was breathless.

Mala collapsed in her arms. "I was so scared, Relle."

"We have to get out. We have to . . ." Ariel looked for Usengu, but he was nowhere in sight. Had he tucked tail and run? Could she be so lucky? She *could not* let him get back to her father's castle with Mala first.

Before Ariel could finish her thought, a net sank into the water over their heads.

A boat bobbed above them.

She gasped.

"MerHunters!" Ariel cried out. She'd been so distracted freeing Mala she hadn't noticed their arrival. "Duck!"

Ariel dragged Mala down deeper into the ocean as the

MerHunters scooped the water with their nets. As she pulled her sister along, she spotted two beady eyes spying on them between a cleft in a rock. Usengu was hiding like the coward he was. He'd set up this meeting, she assumed, and now he needed to deliver. That was his problem, not hers. She was going to get her sister *out* of there!

She was pulling Mala deeper into the water, farther away from the boat, when something caught on her tail. She gazed up at the MerHunters' boat.

"Relle!"

Mala tugged, but Ariel's fin was caught. They had her upside down in the water and were reeling her in. She pulled at the net, trying to undo it from around herself as sharp, jagged claws raked through the water, trying to scoop her and the net up to the surface.

Usengu shot out of shadowed waters, and his fin wrapped around Ariel, shoving her further into the boat's clutches. "Got you!" His eyes flickered with ambition. "For all the trouble you've caused me, now you'll face the same fate as your mother."

He shoved her harder, pushing against her with his full weight, and the closer she got to the surface, the more the nets tightened. "The MerHunters will get their mermaid. I'll get the trident—and eventually control of the sea."

Ariel's chest tightened. She couldn't believe her ears. The

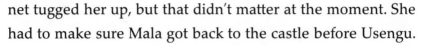

net tugged her up, but that didn't matter at the moment. She had to make sure Mala got back to the castle before Usengu.

"Mala, go, swim! Don't let Usengu get back to Father before you. Take my Fins!"

"I'm not leaving you!" Mala opened her mouth to sing her MerSong in defense, but Usengu clamped a fin around her mouth.

No! Ariel tugged harder at the net, then at her FastFins, as the giant claws swooped toward her again. But it was no use; her Fins were stuck to her, and trapped in the net as she was, she didn't have enough leverage to slip them off. Human hands stretched down from the boat, reaching for her tail. She writhed in the net's grip and wriggled out of the way just as the claws passed, snagging on her bracelet.

The thin twine broke, and the purple pebble snapped off her wrist.

The entire world tipped sideways.

Ariel felt funny all over, dizzy and lightheaded, as the pebble split open like a beam of sunlight and the world around them glowed.

Mala stared, mouth agape in shock. In her head, Ariel could see her mother and herself, like a memory she could touch, just like the memories Silius had shown them. Was this the favor Mother had gone to him for? Had she known that she was in danger and saved a memory for Ariel to find?

In the memory, her mother was humming to her, teaching her some song with words Ariel had never heard before. She was so small she was cradled in Mother's arms. Ariel reached for the memory. The song . . . was that *her* Song? Could it be? Was that what she was seeing? Her throat bobbed with a knot of sorrow. She listened harder, and her heart thrummed as she let the words fill her up. Just *listening* to them, she felt warm and special and different, unlike any feeling she'd had before.

Because . . .

It was . . . *her* MerSong. . . .

Mother *had* had one for her. She'd just been too small to remember that Mother had begun to teach her.

Ariel closed her eyes and pulled at the memory for all she could, holding every word from her mother's mouth, writing it into her heart and her mind. Then she parted her lips and sang like she'd never sung before. Loud, imagining her mother right there with her. She tingled all over as her MerSong filled the ocean around them, shooting out a bright light. She wasn't sure what her Song would do, but it felt right, and if she'd learned anything, it was to trust herself. She sang louder, growing warm all over, the magic of Mother's Song surrounding her. The ocean gleamed so brightly within her Song she thought the sun might have dunked beneath the water. She held each note, with every bit of herself attached to each word, and the world around her shifted. *I'm doing it. I'm really doing it.*

"*Ah!*" Usengu's fins swatted at his eyelids as he fumbled around and bumped into a rock. "Help, I—I can't see!"

Ariel heard wailing from the surface, and a human hand struck the edge of the boat, letting go of the net. Its grip on her loosened, and she started wriggling herself free, blinking against the blinding radiance. Had her MerSong's pulsing bright light done it? Taken their sight? She turned to Mala, who was feeling her way through the water toward her, unable to see as well. *It must have!* And, for better or worse, the Song's effects wouldn't last forever.

Ariel didn't take another second to think. She worked to free herself from the net knotted around her tail as the pebble descended to the ocean floor. She kept singing each and every note, tugging at the threads with fury, unsure how long she could sing without running out of strength. Mala, who'd felt her way over to her, unlooped the last knot from around her.

"That's it!" Mala said. "You did it."

Ariel swished her fin. She was free!

Her lungs burned, begging for a break, but Ariel kept singing. They needed to be far, far away before they would be safe. But she could feel her breath wearing out. *We have to go.* She swam past Usengu, who thrashed, still unable to see, and bumped into the dangling net.

"What's that touching me? Get away from me this minute!" He wriggled and tangled himself into the nets that Ariel had just shed. Ariel couldn't believe her eyes. Her breath hitched as she ran out of wind and her Song petered out.

Usengu blinked, able to see again but fully captured by the MerHunters' binds. He glared at her in rage as the MerHunters pulled, hoisting him up through the water. He tried to fight his way loose, but it was no use. Ariel couldn't look away. She almost felt . . . bad for him? She bit her lip.

"We should go!" Mala rubbed her eyes and tugged Ariel in the direction of home. Her sister was right. Ariel turned to follow but paused when she cupped her bare wrist. The bracelet Mother had given her. Where was it? She scanned the dark ocean below them but saw nothing. She wished she could have held on to it forever, but it was gone and time was short. At least she had its Song etched on her heart.

They dashed off, and the knot in her chest uncinched at the sight of the MerHunters' boat zooming off in the other direction with Usengu on board. She exhaled and swam faster, the pink Coral Moon shining down on them the whole way home.

Chapter 23

The sea felt like a different place after Mala and Ariel returned. The crowd and dignitaries who had sided with Usengu had hung around, waiting to see what would happen and who would return. When Mala and Ariel arrived and told them everything, the whole kingdom seemed to give a collective sigh. She was happy to report that Usengu wouldn't be a bother ever again.

She and her sisters spent that first night back hearing tales from Mala about all she'd been through. How she had confided in Usengu that she'd secretly commissioned a special flora-maker to bring an arrangement to the High Sun palace the morning of the ceremony. So, when Usengu had shown up to her room, she expected to be taken to meet the flora-maker. But he kidnapped her instead. She even opened up about Ieka. Indira and Caspia were the slowest to congratulate her. But they did, and come morning, it felt like the castle moved with new life.

Seven more days passed, and they all stayed in their father's castle together, soaking each other up, making preparations for Ariel's Protector Ceremony, which had been rescheduled now that all was well in the kingdom. The Carinaean palace was done up as beautifully as before. And the whole sea was invited, as Ariel had wanted. And she was glad, because she had *much* to tell them.

But even returning to High Sun felt entirely different. Her mother wasn't there, but all her sisters were. And Ariel knew nothing would come between them anymore. She eyed herself in the looking glass.

"Ready?" Indira said. "On three."

Her sisters wrapped her shawl around her. Her chest felt like it was being squeezed between crocodile jaws from nervousness. Next was the headpiece. Wait, where was her headpiece?

"Oh, sweet Ariel," Julia said, hovering out of the way with a glassy stare. "If your mother could see—" Her housekeeper hid the rest of her words behind a quiet whimper.

"Now how does it feel?" Tamika strung a strand of beads around her neck. "Don't move too fast. You might rip something."

Her sisters, every single one of them, oohed and aahed as she twisted, admiring herself.

"I can move a little, I think. So I'm good." Ariel blinked in disbelief. It was really happening. She was going to be Protector of Carinae.

"Your sisters and I wanted to do something extra special for you." Mala squeezed her shoulders. "We really thought about how hard it must have been not having Mother around through all of this, and yet you still were able to focus on bringing us all together. So we wanted to gift you a little something for today in honor of her."

"Eee! Time for gifts!" Tamika rushed off to grab hers, and Indira approached, her expression pinched in the goofiest grin. She handed Ariel a tiny box wrapped in beautiful ties. "Open it!"

Ariel undid the tie and found a comb beaded with green pearls and dotted with flora. "Oh, my goodness, Indira, it's beautiful. Wherever did you get this?"

"Mother gave it to me. I want you to have it."

Ariel threw her arms around Indira. She couldn't find words to express just how thankful she was. "You all are the absolute best," she said as her sisters swarmed around her to present their gifts one at a time. Caspia's was a shell filled with beauty paint, with tiny rosettes decorating the outside. "Mother gave me this when I broke mine. She said her mother had given it to her, and her mother before her. Now it's yours."

Ariel cupped the shell in her hands and dotted some of its rosy hue on her cheeks. "Caspia, it's so lovely. Thank you."

"Me next!" Perla handed Ariel an oblong gift wrapped in seagrass.

"Oh, Perla, you shouldn't have."

"Oh, hush. You should feel entirely spoiled today. It's your day."

Ariel grinned, pulling a shiny rod out of the grass. "What is it?"

"Honestly, I'm not sure. But shortly after Mother died, Father got rid of all the things she'd collected exploring. One of the maids dropped this as they cleaned out her room, and, well, I kept it. I never figured out what it was for. But . . . I know how much you enjoy baubles, so I thought you'd love it. I think it makes music, somehow?"

"Oh, I do!" Ariel rolled the short rod in her hands and blew through one of its tiny holes. But the stick didn't make a sound. She covered all the holes but one and tried blowing in one end with her nose.

Hummmmm.

"Oh!" She jumped at its weird sound. So that's how it worked. You blew into one end. She'd have to try messing with it again later. "This is really special. Thank you, Perla."

"Okay, now me." Karina handed her a thin circle with an iridescent stone on one end. "Mother gave it to me on my ceremony day. She told me it was for luck. I wore it in my headpiece."

"It's simply beautiful." Ariel held it up to the light, and it shone pink then green then blue. It was almost the width of one of her fingers. "Would you do me the honor?"

Karina took the circle from Ariel and affixed it to her shawl. Tamika was next, and Ariel pinched herself just to be sure this was real. Tamika was actually there with them! She hadn't left since the court meeting, and she and Ariel had spent the better part of the last several nights up late, laughing about the ridiculous things Ariel had gotten into when she was a fry. Like old times. Gosh, she'd missed that. And it was clear—in the departure of Tamika's pallor, the ring of her laughter, the way the light behind her eyes shone bright— that she had missed it, too.

Mala, who hadn't yet gone, approached Ariel with an armful of something sheathed in tarps. "You're more radiant today than you've ever been, Relle. And not because you're dressed up fancy. But because you just look *so* happy." Mala pressed a kiss to Ariel's forehead. "I'm proud of the mermaid you're becoming. And I know Mother would be, too." She handed her the package, and curiosity spurred Ariel's hands to rip it open as fast as she could.

She pulled off the last bit of tarp and gasped. In her lap was a work of art, a sculpted headpiece ornamented with pearls in shades of evening. Golds and pinks; silver tones like ribbons of cloud against a dusky sky. Ariel ran her hands along its details. It was regal and breathtaking and seasoned with age.

"Is this—"

"Yes," Mala said. "It is Mother's headpiece. She wore it when she was crowned. It isn't traditionally what Protectors wear for their ceremonies." She winked. "But Father was willing to make an exception."

Ariel threw her arms around her sister's neck and squeezed tight. What could she ever say to make her understand what this meant to her? She couldn't find words, so she squeezed tighter, and her sweet sister hugged her back. Perla and the rest piled on the hug, and before Ariel knew it, she was swallowed in the center, weighed down in the best possible way by her sisters' adoration and love.

She sniffed, trying to think of some way to convey how much this meant. But none of the words she brought to mind sounded good enough.

"You're *all* here," she managed. "It's like . . . It's like Mother's here, too."

"She is," Mala said. "Through us."

She squeezed them all tighter.

Bum. Bubum. Bum. Bububummm.

The horns were sounding! It was time. "We should probably hurry," Ariel said. "Could you all help me with this headpiece?"

Tamika pinned it down to her hair. Perla touched up Ariel's face. Caspia and Indira dusted off Ariel's shawl. Karina primped Ariel's hair. And Mala pinched Ariel's cheek before they all rushed out the door.

Carinaeans clung to the gates, and the Royal Herald announced their procession as they marched onto a raised dais outside the palace. There was a slew of changes she'd had Father agree to. One was that she would have an escort for her ceremony: her sisters, each and every one of them, together.

One by one they went when their names were called, with Ariel waiting last in line.

"Perla of the Piton Sea," the herald said.

Perla, who was in front of her, turned back and winked before she swam out. "Good luck, sis." The horn blew again, and Ariel knew it was her turn. She swam out and gasped at the sheer extent of the audience. Carinaeans were cheering as far as she could see. She was happy to see their faces. *All their faces.*

Another change she'd been adamant about, which she'd made Father agree to in writing before agreeing to do this Protector thing, was that he had to do away with his plans to segment her territory. Carinae would not be divided; every creature would roam it freely. And once her sisters heard her say it, they followed suit, realizing the way their own views of Sea Monsters had been ill-informed and frankly quite unjust. Each of her sisters requested the king remove the restricted areas in their territories as well. Surprisingly, her father didn't put up a fight. He'd said he'd been reconsidering *much* he'd once hung his crown on.

Just then, her father joined her.

"Thank you again, Father. For listening."

"If only I'd listened sooner."

Sebastian glanced over his shoulder from conducting the puffer band and cleared his throat.

"Oh, and one other thing," her father said. "I've thought about it, and I don't think Sebastian needs to oversee your duties in Carinae after all. You have proved that you are ready all on your own."

"Oh, Father!" She beamed and squeezed him in a hug. Sebastian winked at her, and she felt warm all over.

"Now, shall we begin?" He looped his arm in hers as

Sebastian instructed the band to quiet down. The crowd followed their cue, and Father cleared his throat.

"I'm beyond proud to be here in the beautiful territory of the Carinae Sea today among you loyal and gracious subjects, forgiving subjects, to whom I owe so much, to present my daughter—"

The crowd whooped and hurrahed so loud her father had to raise his voice to be heard.

"Yes, well, I see we all feel the same way about this one here." He smiled, and Ariel's heart leapt. "She is the late queen's and my most stubborn child, to be clear. But in that stubbornness is her surety of self, and the confidence of someone who knows her heart. Carinaeans, you have an extraordinary leader among you. It is with great honor, Ariel, my baby girl, that I hereby proclaim you Protector of a *free* and *boundless* Carinae."

Ariel's insides exploded with excitement. She hugged her father as they were showered in confetti. "Oh, thank you, Father."

"A-RI-ELLE!" the crowd chanted. "A-RI-ELLE!"

"They want to hear from you." Her father gestured for her to take center stage.

She blew out a breath and found Flounder's beaming face in the crowd. She waved at him, and his grin deepened. The crowd's roar blared in her ears, and she couldn't have stopped smiling even if she'd tried to. She skimmed for familiar faces. She spotted Ieka, and right next to him, Mala. Ariel's cheeks pushed up under her eyes. She was grinning so hard she thought her face might pop.

Telling Father about their union hadn't been easy. But Mala did it with firmness so he knew there was no room for argument. His choice was simple: love his daughter and her choices, or lose her. Because she'd made her decision. And it took him a few days, and lots of encouragement from Ariel and the others. But he'd embraced Ieka with a big hug, and the two of them spent that entire evening exchanging tales about how long it took Mala to get ready to go anywhere. Father had much work to do, but it wasn't a bad start.

Ariel cleared her throat and the crowd quieted.

"I'm so grateful to have this opportunity. I won't let you down, Carinae. I—I came into this position with lots of ideas about what it meant, what it would be like. But what I've realized over the last several days as we dealt with our own family tragedy . . ."

In the crowd, Ieka hugged Mala tighter to himself.

"I guess I realized that what makes a community strong isn't a great brain at the helm. No offense, Father."

The crowd laughed.

"But more so, everyone's ability to come together for the

common good of all of us." She eyed Flounder again. "You meet seafolk along the way that have a different take on things. A different set of experiences or way of doing things. And where we find our strength, Carinae, is in our capacity to love"—she found Mala's face in the crowd—"to forgive, to heal"—she winked at Tamika, who was rubbing her wrists—"not in spite of those things, but *because* of them."

She glanced at Father for permission to share the next part, which they'd worked on together in secret as a surprise—not just to Carinae but to Mala and Ieka, especially. A belated wedding gift of sorts. He nodded.

"With that, I have an announcement." In the days leading up to the ceremony, Ariel had made it her business to press Father to, at the very least, rename the Mer–Monster Treaty. But the more she thought about it, the more she realized removing the insensitive language wasn't enough. Because of all she'd done in the search to find Mala and bring Usengu down, her father had given her a free pass to do what she wanted with the Treaty, within reason. So she met with the Sea Monsters and asked them to lay out their concerns. And together, they came up with something utterly ground-breaking. Excitement radiated through her, curling her lips.

"The Mer–Monster Treaty is no longer. It has been replaced with the Sea Protection Pact. The positions of Protector and Resident are no longer for life. Some seafolk may want to get on with their lives and do other things. And that should be okay."

Applause flew up from the crowd. Mala grabbed her face with both hands. She was far from the dais, but Ariel could see her shoulders shaking with joy. She had done it. Her family was back together, stronger than before. They'd found a reason to smile again. Even Father. And to top it all off, her first day as Protector was a huge success.

Ariel smiled, taking in the wondrous world before her. Mother would have been proud she had stayed true to herself and trusted her wanderer's heart. She would do that from now on.

Whatever was to come.

She gazed up at the glowing sun sparkling above a whole unexplored world above the water. *If Father was wrong about Sea Monsters . . . what else could he be wrong about?* Time would tell. Hopefully, next time, he'd listen.

Epilogue

Far away in her ocean lair, Ursula glared through her crystal ball at the crowd cheering for Ariel. Triton wrapped his arm around her shoulders. *Ugh.* She knocked the crystal ball aside, its glass shattering against the walls of her cave. The sight of King Triton, so happy and proud as he looked upon his kingdom, sickened her. *Why did I put that sly Usengu in charge in the first place?* She shouldn't have trusted him with something so important.

They'd had an agreement: kidnap Mala, stir unrest among the Sea Monsters, and let her do the rest. She'd told the MerHunters where to find a whole nest of mermaids.

But they didn't trust her, especially after their buddies had crashed in the Saithe Sea. So she offered them one mermaid, and if she came through on her promise, they'd take her up on the location of an alleged mermaid castle full of a bunch of them.

When Triton had wagered his trident, she could practically see Usengu's eyes glittering with desire. His ambition had gotten the better of him as Triton began to lean on him more and more. He'd been seduced by opportunity, she guessed, to garner more power for himself instead of helping her acquire the throne. *He wanted it for himself.* Ursula bit down, warm with fury.

"Almost had me, that snake," she muttered. It was behind her. She could focus on her revenge and, this time, handle things herself.

"That self-important king can't possibly think he can just banish me and get away with it!" Her voice ricocheted off the walls of her lair. She rubbed her tentacles together, pondering the little mermaid, Ariel. Free-spirited, trusting, and so open-minded . . . A smile curled Ursula's lips. King Triton would pay dearly for shunning her. She glided into the potion chamber of her lair.

Let the plotting begin.

Acknowledgments

What an incredibly historic opportunity this was! I am truly honored and so grateful to have had the privilege to pen the *first ever* young adult novel with a brown-skinned Ariel with locs! *The Little Mermaid*'s star was my favorite princess for so many years as a child. I related so much to her love of collecting things and learning about places she'd never been. So to be able to put together this prequel to the live-action film with the incredible team at Disney was an absolute dream come true. Thank you to the entire team at Disney on both the studio and publishing side!

As always, first, thank you to God, who keeps my fingers moving over these keys. Thank you to my husband for supporting me through this publishing dream, tirelessly and with lots of Crumbl cookies and ice cream. Thank you to my children, Mariah, Daniel, and Sarah Grace, who flipped out, in the best way, when they heard about this project. Your excitement inspired me to say yes in the first place.

Thank you, *thank you*, THANK YOU to Holly Rice, my brilliant editor and fellow Longhorn for reaching out after meeting Rue and Tasha with the challenge of penning this sister-driven story. *Seven* sisters, PHEW! Ha ha, but look, we did it! You have been such a joy to work with! Thank you for always listening—*and* hearing—because those are different. <3

Thank you to my incredible agent, Jodi Reamer, and the Writers House team. I tell you this all the time, but you changed my life! So grateful to have you in my corner. Huge thanks to Emily Golden, who is always there for every single word with encouragement and extraordinary CP feedback. Thank you for sharing my brain and loving me through all of my projects, ha ha. Thank you to Jessica F, Jessica L, Ayana G, Jessica O, Deborah F, Ronnie D, Stephanie J, Tami C, Kelis R, Mary R, and others who let me squeal about this project before the world could know, who entertained my excitement over scant details, and who were there to encourage me to get words down when I was running out of steam.

Thank you to my forever cheerleaders who root for me endlessly, Nic, Sabaa, Dhonielle, Alexa, and so many others. I love you all!

I'm so grateful to sweet friends who know nothing about publishing, ha ha, but squeal, jumping up and down anytime I have book news and shout about it to everyone they know. Diarra, Alyssa, Andrea G, Kelle S, Paige A, Natasha B, Jennifer P, Wendy C, Kim W, Laura W, Amy D (and your sweet parents), Bill, Chris, Sue, and so many more! (Mary, Martha, May, I can't wait for you all to read this!)

To my family who loves me endlessly and always supports me: Mommy, Paigey, Nae, Roslyn, Rocqell, Aunty Regina, Sydney, Micah, Aunt Jackie, Uncle Chuck for filling the gap, I could never do anything without all of you guys' love and support. (We got a *Black* Ariel, y'all! Like WHAT?! Eeee!)

And the most special thank you to Grandpa Eaglin, who is my rock, who, at this moment in life, is carrying the lessons on grief on these pages squarely on his shoulders. You are my beacon, Paw Paw. I could not have explored the deep waters of Ariel's grief (as I literally am living it on my own right now, too) without you by my side. You inspire me every day and remind me that ultimately: **grief is love persevering**. (Someone much wiser than me coined that phrase.)

There are so many people who have had their hands on this project that I may never have the chance to meet, but please know that I am grateful for every read, every in-line comment, every glance over, every sketch of cover design. Thank you! Partnering with you all has been an honor.